THE HAMMER TOUCH

Velda wasn't at her desk. Her pocketbook sat there and a paper cup of coffee had spilled over and stained the sheaf of paper before dripping to the floor. And I didn't have to move far before I saw her body crumpled up against the wall, half her face a mass of clotted blood.

The door to my office was partially open and there was somebody still in there. I couldn't play it smart. I had to explode, and rammed through the door ready to blow somebody into a death full of bloody, flying parts. . . .

That was how it began. Then it got really rough. . . .

THE KILLING MAN

"Mickey Spillane is one of the best-selling writers of our time . . . Mike Hammer is an icon of our culture."
—*The New York Times*

PREVIOUS BOOKS BY MICKEY SPILLANE

I, the Jury
My Gun Is Quick
Vengeance Is Mine
One Lonely Night
The Big Kill
The Long Wait
Kiss Me, Deadly
The Deep
The Girl Hunters
The Snake
Day of the Guns
Bloody Sunrise
The Death Dealers
The Twisted Thing
The By-Pass Control
The Body Lovers
The Delta Factor
Survival Zero
The Last Cop Out
The Erection Set

The Killing Man
Mickey Spillane

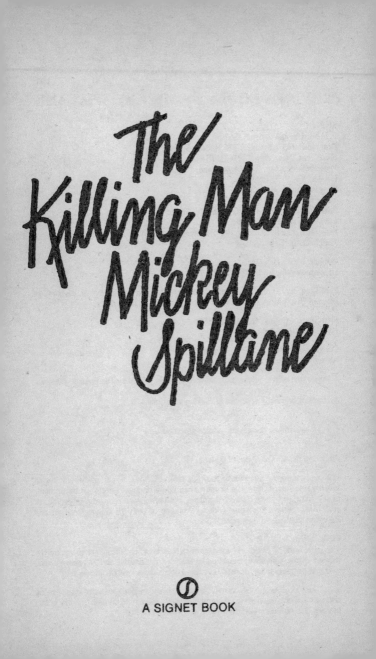

A SIGNET BOOK

SIGNET
Published by the Penguin Group
Penguin Books USA Inc., 375 Hudson Street,
New York, New York 10014, U.S.A.
Penguin Books Ltd, 27 Wrights Lane,
London W8 5TZ, England
Penguin Books Australia Ltd, Ringwood,
Victoria, Australia
Penguin Books Canada Ltd, 2801 John Street,
Markham, Ontario, Canada L3R 1B4
Penguin Books (N.Z.) Ltd, 182–190 Wairau Road,
Auckland 10, New Zealand

Penguin Books Ltd, Registered Offices:
Harmondsworth, Middlesex, England

Published by Signet, an imprint of New American Library, a division of
Penguin Books USA Inc. Previously published in a Dutton edition.

First Signet Printing, November, 1990
10 9 8 7 6 5 4 3 2 1

A signed first edition of this book has been privately printed by The Franklin Library.

An excerpt originally appeared in *Playboy* magazine.

REGISTERED TRADEMARK—MARCA REGISTRADA

Printed in the United States of America

PUBLISHER'S NOTE
This is a work of fiction. Names, characters, places, and incidents either are the
product of the author's imagination or are used fictitiously, and any resemblance
to actual persons, living or dead, events, or locales is entirely coincidental.

*To Jane
with love*

 **1**

Some days hang over Manhattan like a huge pair of unseen pincers, slowly squeezing the city until you can hardly breathe. A low growl of thunder echoed up the cavern of Fifth Avenue and I looked up to where the sky started at the seventy-first floor of the Empire State Building. I could smell the rain. It was the kind that hung above the orderly piles of concrete until it was soaked with dust and debris and when it came down it wasn't rain at all, but the sweat of the city.

When I reached my corner I crossed against the light and ducked into the ground-level arcade of my office building. It wasn't often that I bothered coming in at all on Saturday, but the client couldn't make it any other time except noon today, and from what Velda had told me, he was representing some pretty big interests.

Two others were waiting for the elevator, one an architect in the penthouse suite and the other a delivery boy from the deli down the street. Both of them looked bored and edgy. The day had gotten to them, too. When the elevator arrived, we got in, I punched my button and rode it up to the eighth floor.

On an ordinary day the corridor would have been filled with the early lunch crowd, but now the emptiness gave the place an eerie feeling, as though I were a trespasser and hidden eyes were watching me. Except that I was the only one there and the single sign of life was the light behind my office door.

I turned the knob, pushed it open and just stood there a second because something was wrong, sure as hell wrong, and the total silence was as loud as a wild scream. I had the .45 in my hand, crouched and edged to one side, listening, waiting, watching.

Velda wasn't at her desk. Her pocketbook sat there and a paper cup of coffee had spilled over and stained the sheaf of papers before dripping to the floor. And I didn't have to move far before I saw her body crumpled up against the wall, half her face a mass of clotted blood that seeped from under her hair.

The door to my office was partially open and

there was somebody still in there, sitting at my desk, part of his arm clearly visible. I couldn't play it smart. I had to explode and rammed through the door in a blind fury ready to blow somebody into a death full of bloody, flying parts ... then stopped, my breath caught in my throat, because it had already been done.

The guy sitting there had been taped to my chair, his body immobilized. The wide splash of adhesive tape across his mouth had immobilized his voice too, but all the horror that had happened was still there in his glazed, dead eyes that stared at hands whose fingertips had been amputated at the first knuckle and lay in neat order on the desk top. A dozen knife slashes had cut open the skin of his face and chest and his clothes were a sodden mass of congealed blood.

But the thing that killed him was the note spike I had kept my expense receipts on. Somebody had slipped them all off the six-inch steel nail, positioned it squarely in the middle of the guy's forehead and pounded it home with the bronze paperweight that held my folders down. And the killer left a note, but I didn't stop to read it.

Velda's pulse was weak, but it was there, and when I lifted her hair there was a huge hematoma above her ear, the skin split wide from the vicious swelling of it. Her breathing was shallow and her vital signs weren't good at all. I grabbed her coat off the rack, draped it around her, stood up and forced the rage to leave me, then found the number in my phone book and dialed it.

The nurse said, "Dr. Reedey's office."

"Meg, this is Mike Hammer," I told her. "Burke in?"

"Yes, but—"

"Listen, call an ambulance and get a stretcher up here right away and get Burke to come up *now*. Velda has been hurt badly."

"An accident?"

"No. She was attacked. Somebody tried to smash her skull."

While she dialed she said, "Don't move her. I'll send the doctor right up. Keep her warm and . . ." I hung up in midsentence.

Pat Chambers wasn't at home, but his message service said he could be reached at his office. The sergeant at the switchboard answered, took my name, put me through and when Pat said, "Captain Chambers," I told him to get to my office with a body bag. I wasn't about to waste time with explanations while Velda could be dying right beside me.

I was helpless, unable to do anything except kneel there, hold her hand and speak to her. Her skin was clammy and her pulse was getting weaker. The frustration I felt was the kind you get in a dream when you can't run fast enough to get away from some terror that is chasing you. And now I had to stay here and watch Velda slip away from life while some bastard was out there getting farther and farther away all the time.

There were hands around my shoulders that yanked me back away from her and Burke said, "Come on, Mike, let me get to her."

I almost swung on him before I realized who he was and when he saw my face he said, "You all right?"

After a moment I said, "I'm all right," and moved back out of the way.

Burke Reedey was a doctor who had come out of the slaughter of Vietnam with all the expertise needed to handle an emergency like this. He and his nurse moved swiftly and the helpless feeling I'd had before abated and I moved the desk to give him room, trying not to listen to their comments. There was something in their tone of voice that had a desperate edge to it. Almost on cue the ambulance attendants arrived, visibly glad to see a doctor there ahead of them, and carefully they got Velda onto the stretcher and out of the office, Burke going with them.

All that time Meg had very carefully steered me to one side, obscuring my vision purposely, realizing what was going through my mind, and when they had left she handed me a glass of water and offered me a capsule from a plastic container.

I shook my head. "Thanks, but I don't need anything."

She put the cap back on the container. "What happened, Mike?"

"I don't know yet." I pointed to the door of my office. "Go look in there."

A worried look touched her eyes and she walked to the door and opened it. I didn't think old-time nurses could gasp like that. Her hand went to her mouth and I saw her head shake in horror. "Mike . . . you didn't mention . . ."

"He's dead. Velda wasn't. The cops will take care of that one."

She backed away from the door, turned and looked at me. "That's the first . . . deliberate murder . . . I've ever seen." Slowly, very slowly, her eyes widened.

I shook my head. "No, I didn't do it. Whoever hit Velda did that too."

The relief in her expression was plain. "Do you know why?"

"Not yet."

"You *have* called the police, haven't you?"

"Right after I spoke to you." I nodded toward the door. "Why don't you go back to the office. I'll take care of things here."

"The doctor thought I should look after you."

"I'm okay. If I weren't I'd tell you. The cops will want to speak to both you and Burke later but there's no use of you getting all tied up with them now."

"You're sure?"

I nodded. "Just stay with Velda, will you?"

"As soon as the doctor calls I'll check in with you."

When she left I walked over to the miniature bar by the window and picked up a glass. Hell, this was no time to take a drink. I put the glass back and went into my office.

The dead guy was still looking at his mutilated hands, seemingly ignoring the spike driven into his skull until the ornamental base of it indented his skin. The glaze over his eyes seemed thicker.

For the first time I looked at the note on my desk, the large capital letters printed almost triumphantly across a sheet of my letterhead under the logo. It read, YOU DIE FOR KILLING ME. Beneath it, in deliberately fine handwriting, was the signature, *Penta.*

I heard the front door open and Pat shouted my name. I called back, "In here, Pat."

Pat was a cop who had seen it all. This one was just another on his list. But the kill wasn't what disturbed him. It was where it happened. He turned to the uniform at the door. "Anybody outside?"

"Only our people. They're shortstopping everybody at the elevators."

"Good. Keep everybody out for five minutes," he told a cop who stood in the doorway. "Our guys too."

"Got it," the cop said and turned away.

"Let's talk," Pat said.

It didn't take long. "I was to meet a prospective client named Bruce Lewison at noon in my office. Velda went ahead to open up and get some other work out of the way. I walked in a few minutes before twelve and found her on the floor and the guy dead."

"And you touched nothing?"

"Not in here, Pat. I wasn't about to wait for you to show before I got a doctor for Velda."

Pat looked at me with that same old look.

I could feel a twist in my grin. There was nothing funny about it. "Oh, I'll get to the bastard, Pat. Sooner or later."

"Cut that shit, will you?"

"Sure."

"You know this guy?"

I shook my head. "He's new to me."

"Somebody thought he was killing you, pal."

"We don't look alike at all."

"He was in your chair."

"Yeah, that he was."

He was looking at the note and said, "Who *did* you kill, Mike?"

I said, "Come on Pat. Don't play games."

"This note mean anything to you?"

"No. I *don't* know why, but somebody sure was serious about it."

"Okay," he said. His eyes looked tired. "Let's get our guys in here."

While the photographer shot the corpse from all angles and did closeups on the mutilation, Pat and I went into Velda's office where the

plainclothes officers dusted for prints and vacuumed the area for any incidental evidence. Pat
had already jotted down what I had told him.
Now he said, "Give me the entire itinerary of
your day, Mike. Start from when you got up this
morning and I'll check everything out while it's
fresh."

"Look ... when Velda comes around ..." I
saw the look on Pat's face and nodded. My stomach was all knotted up and all I wanted was to
breathe some fresh, cold air.

"I got up at seven. I showered, dressed and
went down to the deli for some rolls, picked up
the paper, went back to the apartment, ate, read
the news and took off for the gym."

"Which one?"

"Bing's Gym. You know where it is. I got there
at nine thirty, put in a little better than an hour
in the exercise room, showered and checked out
at eleven thirty. Bing can verify that himself. It
was a twenty-minute walk to the office and on
the way I saw two people I knew. One was Bill
Sheen, the beat cop, the other was Manuel Florio
who owns the Pompeii Bar on Sixth Avenue. We
walked together for a block, then split. I got to
the office a few minutes before twelve and walked
into ... this." I waved my hand at the room.
"Burke Reedey will give you his medical report
on Velda and the ME will be able to pinpoint a
time of death pretty well, so don't get me mixed
up in suspect status."

Pat finished writing, tore a leaf out of the pad and closed the book. He called one of the detectives over and handed him the slip, telling him to check out all the details of my story. "Let's just keep straight with the system, buddy. Face it, you're not one of its favorite people."

The assistant medical examiner was a tubby little guy with light blue eyes that bristled with curiosity. Every detail was a major item and when he was finished with the physical aspect of the examination, he stepped back, walked around the body slowly, seeming to do a psychological analysis of the crime. Pat didn't try to interrupt him. This was the ME's moment and whatever he could garner from his inspection now would be valuable because the body would never be seen in this position again. Twice he went back to do a close scrutiny of the desk spike in the dead man's forehead, then made a satisfied grimace and snapped his bag shut.

Pat asked, "What do you think?"

"About the time?"

"Yes, for one thing."

The ME looked at his watch. "I would say that he was killed between ten and eleven o'clock. Certainly not after eleven. I will be more specific after the postmortem. Has he been identified?"

"Not yet," Pat said.

"An interesting death. Those facial and chest

cuts seem to have been made with an extremely sharp, short-bladed instrument."

"Penknife?" I asked him.

"Yes, possibly. Some people carry things like that."

"Any medical reasons for the slashings?"

"Want me to speculate?"

"Certainly," Pat said.

"Those were made to terrorize the victim. It's amazing what the sight of a blade opening up his own body can do to a person's psyche. Those wounds are too deep to be superficial, yet not deep enough to be fatal."

"And that brings us to the hands."

"A very unusual disfiguration." His bright blue eyes looked at both of us, then settled on Pat. "Have you ever seen this before?" Pat shook his head. "Someplace I recall hearing of this happening. I'll do a little research on it when I get back to the office. Frankly, I think it's a signature stratagem."

"A what?"

"Something a killer leaves to remember him by."

I said, "That's a pretty complicated way of writing your name."

"Agreed," the ME nodded, "but you'll never forget it. But the one he was impressing it on was the victim himself. Look, let me show you how he did this." He took the dead man's arm, stiff with rigor mortis, forcing the hand with the forefinger out and the other knuckles bent down, against the desk. Where the finger ended you could see the cut of the blade in the wood. "Imagine having to watch as each finger was cut off at the knuckle and not even being able to scream for relief? The pain must have been incredible, but even then, it could not have been as bad as the final act of hammering that spike into his head."

"What are you saving for last, Doctor?"

The ME gave Pat a sage little smile. "You're wondering how a grown man would let himself be totally immobilized like that?"

"Right on," Pat told him.

Swinging the swivel chair around so the back of the corpse's head faced us, the ME lifted up the shaggy hair and fingered a small lump over the ear. "A tap with the usual blunt instrument, hard enough to render the victim unconscious for ten minutes or so."

My mouth went dry and something felt like it was crawling up my back. The one he had laid on Velda wasn't to knock her out. That one was a killing blow, one swung with deliberate, murderous intent. I looked at the phone again. Meg still hadn't called.

Pat bent over and examined the body carefully. His arm brushed the dead man's coat and pushed it open. Sticking up out of the shirt pocket was a Con Edison bill folded in half. When Pat straightened it out he looked at the name and said, "Anthony Cica." He held it out for me to look at. "You know him, Mike?"

"Never saw him before." His address was on the Lower East Side of Manhattan.

"You're lucky you had a stand-in."

"Too bad Velda didn't have one." The tightness ran up me again and I began to breathe hard without knowing it.

Pat was shaking my arm. "Come off it, Mike."

I wiped the back of my hand across my mouth and nodded.

The ME was pointing toward the note. "And that's his ego trip, wouldn't you say? The dead man can't read, so who will? And who is Penta?"

"You're leaving all the fun stuff for us, Doc."

"Keep me informed. I'm very interested. You'll get my report tomorrow." As he went to pass me he stopped and gave me those blue eyes again. "Do I know you, sir?"

"Mike Hammer," I told him.

"I've heard mention of you."

"This is my office," I said.

"Yes." He looked around, curiously critical. "Who is your decorator?"

"That's his sense of humor," Pat said when the ME left. Then he went over and called in two of his people to go over the corpse itself.

I went to the phone and called Meg. The answering service said she would be back at six. I called the hospital directly, but there was no report on Velda's condition so far. Nobody would speculate.

It was another hour before the specialists finished and the body was carted out in its rubberized shroud. Pat was on the phone and when he hung up he turned to me and said tiredly, "The papers just got wind of it. They still on your side?"

"Hell, most of the old guys are buddies, but some of those young ones are weirdos."

"Wait till they read that note."

"Yeah, great."

"You still haven't told me who you killed, Mike." This time there was a quiet seriousness in his tone. It was a question direct and simple.

I turned and faced him, meeting his eyes square on. "Anybody I ever took down you know about. The last one was Julius Marco, the son of a bitch who was about to kill that kid when I nailed him, and that was four years ago."

"How many have you shot since?"

"A few. None died."

"You testified in a couple of Murder One cases, didn't you?"

"Sure. So did a few other people."

"Recently?"

"Hell, no. The last one was a few years back."

"Then who would want you dead?"

"Nobody I can think of."

"Hell, somebody wants you even better than dead. They want you all chopped up and with a spike through your head. Somebody had a business engagement with you at noon, got here early, took out Velda and didn't have to wait for you because there was a guy in your office he thought was you and he nailed that poor bastard instead."

"I've thought of that," I said.

"And we're stuck until we get IDs on everybody and a statement from Velda."

"Looks like that," I told him. "You through here?"

"Yeah."

"Sealing the place up?"

Pat shrugged. "No need to."

I picked up the phone again and called the building super. I told him what had happened and that I needed the place cleaned up. He said he'd do it personally. I thanked him and hung up.

Pat said, "Let's go get something to eat. You'll feel better. Then we'll go to the hospital."

"No sense in that. Velda was unconscious and in critical condition. No visitors. I'll tell you what you can do though."

"What's that?"

"Station a cop at her door. That Penta character missed two of us and he just might want another go at somebody when he finds out what happened."

Pat picked up the phone in Velda's office and relayed the message. When he hung up he said to me, "What are your plans?"

"Hell, I'm going to Anthony Cica's apartment with you."

"Listen, Mike . . ."

"You don't want me to go alone, do you?"

"Man, you're a real pisser," Pat said.

Outside it was barely raining. It was more like the sky was spitting at us. It was ending up the way it had started. Bad, real bad.

Pat had an unmarked car at the curb and we drove across town and headed south on Second Avenue. The pavements were slick, brightly alive with neon reflections and the broad streaks of dimmed headlights. The weather meant nothing to the people who lived here. They never were out in it long enough to annoy them. Pat didn't bother with his red light, simply moving in and out of the stream of yellow cabs and occasional cars with automatic precision.

Both of us stayed pretty deep in our thoughts until I mentioned, "You could have had one of the detectives do this."

"Don't get hairy on me, pal. I'm not letting you alone on any primary investigation."

"You're investigating a corpse, not a murder suspect. What the hell could I do?"

The car in front of us hit the brakes and Pat swore at the driver and cut to the left. "I don't know what you could do, Mike. There's no telling what's ever going to happen with you. There's something that hangs over you like a magnet that pulls all the crazies right to your door."

"No crazy did this."

"Any killer is crazy," he stated.

"Maybe, but some are more deliberate than others."

Pat slowed and turned left, checked the numbers on the buildings when he could find one, then counted down to the tenement he was looking for. Hardly anybody in this area owned a car and whoever did wouldn't park it on the street. We parked behind a stripped wreck of an old Buick and got out of the car.

A lot of years ago they talked of condemning areas like this but never got around to it. One by one the buildings lost any rental benefits and were abandoned by their owners. Here and there were a few that somebody had renovated enough to warrant having paying tenants as long as they didn't mind sharing the space with roaches and rats.

We went up the sandstone stoop and pushed through the scarred wooden doors. The vestibule light in the ceiling was protected by a wire cage, a forty-watter that turned everything a sickly yellow. As usual, the brass mailbox doors were all sprung open, each one with a cheap paper circular stuck in it. Scrawled on the top of the brass frame were names in black marker ink. The middle two were half rubbed out. Anthony Cica was the one who had the top floor.

The inner vestibule light only went halfway up the stairs, but Pat had a pocket power light

with him and lit our way up among the litter
that spilled down the stairs. We stepped over a
couple of empty beer cans and some half-pint
whiskey bottles to get to the first landing. Apparently visitors never got above the top steps. The
rest of the way was clear. The door we were
looking for had the number four drawn on it in
white paint. It was locked. In fact, it had three
locks on it.

"Think a credit card can get them open, Pat?"

"Hell no. I have a warrant."

"Then use it."

He kicked the door panel out, reached in and
opened the locks, then pushed it open with his
foot. Standing to one side, he felt for the light
switch beside the jamb, found it and flipped it
on. Nothing moved except the roaches.

The occupant hadn't been a total slob. There
were no dirty dishes and the sink was clean. The
furniture was old, probably secondhand, the bed
wasn't made, simply straightened out a little,
and the small bathroom had a semblance of order
to it. The refrigerator belonged in a museum, but
it still worked, the unit on its top humming away.
In it were two frozen dinners, half a carton of
milk, some butter and a six-pack of beer.

I said, "What do you think?"

"Permanent quarters. Lousy, but fixed."

Three suits and a sports jacket hung in the
closet, all several years old. Two pairs of shoes,
one brown, the other black, were on the floor

beside a piece of Samsonite luggage that was open and empty. In the corner, almost out of sight, was a small metal rectangle. I picked it up with a handkerchief.

"Pat . . ."

He came over and I showed him the clip for an automatic. It was loaded with 7.65-millimeter cartridges.

"Nice," he muttered. "Let's find the rest of it."

We looked, but that was all there was. No gun was around to fit the clip. Pat said, "That's damned strange."

"Not necessarily. It was kicked in the corner of the closet. It could have been there before he moved in. I almost missed it."

In fifteen minutes we had covered every inch of the place. A cardboard box on one of the shelves held a few dozen receipted bills, some paycheck slips and a stack of old two-dollar betting slips from a Jersey track. It was a stupid souvenir, but at least he could count his losses.

The only thing that didn't seem to belong there was a handmade toolbox with a collection of chisels, bits and two hammers with well-worn handles. Pat said, "These tools are antiques, all made by Sergeant Hardware back in the twenties." He fondled one of the long, thin blades, feeling the sharpness with a fingertip. "Somebody did precision work with these babies. Real sculpture."

"Think they're stolen?"

"What for? No fast cash value in it. Looks more like a keepsake to me." He turned the box upside down. Neatly carved into the bottom were the initials V.D.

"You'd better handle that with rubber gloves." I grinned.

"I'll get a penicillin shot later." He gave the place a last look around. "Anthony Cica didn't leave much of a legacy. I wonder who inherits?"

I was fitting the broken panel back in the hole Pat's foot had made. "Well, take the toolbox for whoever the relative is. Nothing else is worthwhile."

He shut off the light and closed the door. When we felt our way down the stairs and got to the street we stood there a minute, both wondering what would make a guy like Anthony Cica live in a place like this, his only treasure an antique toolbox.

Pat finally hunched his shoulders against the rain and we got into the car. Deliberately, he looked across at me. "That killer couldn't have wanted Cica, Mike."

"Why the hell would he want me?"

He started the car. "Guess we'll have to find that out."

2

It was a dreamless night, but I awoke tired. I felt as if I had been running and to awaken was an effort. Only for a few seconds was there a blankness in time before the whole scenario of the day before came crashing down in front of me.

My hand grabbed for the phone and I hit the buttons for the hospital. I was overanxious, got the wrong number and had to hit them again. This time the switchboard put me through to the nurse on Velda's floor. Calmly, she told me Velda had had a quiet night, was still in critical condition, but improving. No, she could have no visitors yet.

The relief I felt was like a cool wave of water

washing over me. Hospitals never wanted to sound optimistic, so the report was a favorable one. I called Burke Reedey at home and got him out of bed. All he could say was "Damn it, I've been up all night. Who is this?"

"It's Mike, Burke. What's with Velda?"

"Oh," he said. "You. Wait a minute." I heard him pour something, heard him swallow it, then he said, "She had a close one that time. One hell of a concussion. That blow was delivered with enough force to kill her, but her hair bunched under the instrument and blunted the impact. I was afraid we'd find a fracture there but we didn't. All her vital signs are coming up and we're keeping her isolated for another day."

"She regain consciousness?"

"About four this morning. It was just a brief awakening and she went back to sleep."

"When can I see her?"

"Probably this evening, but I want no communication. She is going to be highly sedated or have one hell of a headache. Either way she won't want to talk."

"What was she hit with?"

"Someday they'll find another term for the usual 'blunt instrument.' However, it wasn't a hard object like a pipe. This had a soft crushing effect and from what I've seen of leather black-jacks, this was what her attacker used. Incidentally, this is what I gave the police in my report."

He paused a moment, then went on: "Meg told me there was a dead man in the other office."

"Burke, you couldn't have helped. He was real dead. Velda was alive and that's all that counted."

"You're a sentimental bastard, you know that?"

"Just realistic, pal."

"I want to know what this is all about."

"You'll get it."

"I hope so. You're the only excitement I ever get anymore."

"Excitement I don't need," I told him. "And Burke . . ."

"Yeah?"

"Thanks."

"No trouble. You'll get a bill."

I hung up, made coffee in the kitchen and had a leftover roll from yesterday. When I turned on the news I had to wait fifteen minutes before local events came on and the announcer mentioned a torture murder in the office of a Manhattan businessman. The case was under investigation and no names were made public. As yet, the victim was unidentified.

I just finished pouring my second cup of coffee when the phone rang. Pat said, "I think you ought to come on down to my office."

"What's happening?"

"For one thing, we had an ID on our victim."

"What's the other?"

"We have some strange company here."

"Bad?"

"It's not good."

"Well. I'll change my underwear," I said. After the good news from the hospital, nothing was going to spoil my day.

Sunday morning in New York is like no other time. From dawn until ten the city is like an unborn fetus. There are small sounds and stirrings that are hardly noticeable, then little movements take place and forms emerge, but nothing is *happening*. It is a time when you could get anywhere quickly and quietly because of the strange emptiness.

The lonely cabbie who picked me up would be going off shift shortly and, fortunately, didn't want to talk. He took me to Pat's building, took my money, switched on the OFF DUTY light and went back uptown.

Sunday had even infiltrated the police department. On the ground floor it was coffee-and-doughnuts time with a minimum crew at work. Everybody was friendly including Sergeant Klaus who winked and told me Captain Chambers and company were expecting me upstairs.

Pat was in the corridor when I got off the elevator and without a word, steered me into his office. When he closed the door he said, "You told me you didn't know the guy who got killed."

"That's right, I didn't."

Something had hold of Pat and he was mad. "You sure?"

"Look, Pat, what's the deal here? I told you I didn't know him."

"He was a delivery guy from a stationery store who brought up some letterhead samples for you to okay."

"Velda took care of that stuff."

"The guy called the store and told the boss to go ahead with the order."

"So that's what he was doing at my desk. You get the time?"

"Around ten twenty or so."

"That fixes it then."

"But there's a little more to it."

"Oh?"

"His name was Anthony DiCica. Mean anything to you?"

I shook my head. "So someplace he dropped the 'Di' part of his name."

"Seems that way."

"That accounts for the V.D. initials on that toolbox. It must have been his old man's. So where does that leave us?"

"We have a package on him in New York. He went down twice for minor crimes fifteen years ago. Petty stuff, but at least he has a record. That much we got when we ran his driver's license through."

"How about prints?"

"Those first knuckle joints came back from the lab this morning. We rolled them and got them on the computers."

"Then what's on your mind, Pat?"

"Usually we can handle our own homicides here without any interference. Suddenly some first-class interest shows up . . . the DA's office."

I shrugged. "So, he's got a right."

"This is not a general occurrence, pal. When I got back here word had already come down. That note stays confidential until the DA decides to release it. What I think shook them up is that signature, Penta. Hell, it couldn't've been anything else."

"What did they give you on it?"

"They gave me a lot of shit, that's all. I raised hell upstairs, but when the inspector says to go along, we go along."

I gave Pat a friendly rap on the shoulder. "If those squirrels want to play games, let them. A nice screwball case like this can make some interesting headlines."

"Their attitude stinks, Mike." He paused, then glanced at me anxiously. "You mention that note at all?"

"This is the first time I've been on something that the newshounds weren't all over me. Between this being the weekend and my office on the eighth floor where you could contain those guys, it was a pretty damn quiet murder. How many others did you have last night?"

"Four in Manhattan."

"So we got lost in the crowd."

"Not for long, boy, not for long. I can smell

this one about to bust open like an abscessed tooth."

"It's a weirdo."

"Weirdo my ass. Wait until you see who wants to meet you."

"Oh?"

"We have a new assistant district attorney who wants to speak to you. With her is somebody from the governor's office in Albany. He has a pretty heavy letter on embossed stationery that requests we give him full cooperation."

"And that he gets."

"Certainly," Pat acknowledged. "Let's go meet your enemy."

New York City has numerous assistant district attorneys, but they aren't numbered in order of rank or seniority so they can all sound like the top dog on the block. Candace Amory was far from being a dog.

She was a tall patrician-looking blonde with a cover-girl face and a body that didn't just happen. Every bit of her was carefully cultivated and when she moved you knew she danced and could ski and in the water could take two-hundred-foot dives in scuba gear. The high-breasted look she had was for real, enhanced by a suit so dramatically underplayed in spectacular design that it reeked of money that could buy whatever it wanted.

You would never call Candace Amory "Candy." You would want to kiss the lusciousness of those full lips until the thought occurred that it might be like putting your tongue on a cold sled runner and never being able to get it off.

One day I would like to catch her off base and tag her with a ball where she would never forget.

In that one second our eyes touched she knew everything I was thinking and knew I realized it as well. I nodded and said, "Miss Amory," and held out my hand. It wasn't lack of etiquette, just a challenge she met without any change of expression at all. I knew she would have a good grip and let her feel mine too.

"Mr. Hammer," she said. Her voice even matched the rest of her. Throaty, but not altogether soft. There was a firmness there. A tiny Phi Beta Kappa pin was suspended on a fine golden chain around her neck, nestling between her breasts.

There was a dominance about her that she was exuding like an invisible veil and I smiled, just barely smiled with my eyes licking hers, and for an instant there was the minutest change of expression, the cat suddenly realizing the mouse was a cobra, and the veil was sucked back in.

The man from Albany was Jerome Coleman and he didn't specify what his position was. But he was official, he looked legal and he could have been a cop. We said a brief hello and took Pat's offer to sit down around the small conference table. The chair I was offered made me the target for all remarks, so I ignored it and sat in the one next to it. If somebody wanted to fence me in they had better book me first. I saw Pat suppress a smile and Coleman seem annoyed. Miss Amory knew I did it deliberately and just as deliberately took the seat opposite me.

"Who starts?" I said.

Jerome Coleman felt inside his jacket and took out a folded sheet of paper and spread it out in front of him. It was upside down, but I saw it was a copy of the note left on my desk by the killer. "We don't like enigmas, Mr. Hammer."

I kept my mouth shut and waited.

Miss Amory said, "You seem to be implicated in a murder. The alibi you gave Captain Chambers checked out, so you weren't involved with participation in the killing, but nevertheless, you seem to be a principal in the act."

"I'm glad you said *seem*."

She ignored my remark. "Apparently the victim was mistaken for you and horribly brutalized. If that was an act of vengeance, the killer certainly must have had a reason."

"Miss Amory," I said, "I'm glad you didn't read me my rights."

"You're not being arrested, Mr. Hammer."

"This is a direct interrogation, you know."

"Quite so. And you are a licensed private investigator under the laws of New York State, with a permit to carry a weapon and expected to be in full compliance with the laws and statutes of this state and to cooperate fully in assisting in their enforcement."

There was nothing I had to crawl out from under, so I smiled that little smile again. "What can I tell you?"

"The note has reference to you killing somebody," she said.

"The note has reference to me killing the killer," I reminded her.

"And that is the enigma," Coleman put in. His finger underlined the capitalized YOU DIE FOR KILLING ME.

So far Pat had said nothing. He was letting me carry the ball. "Mr. Coleman . . . I've never been indicted for murder. Nor for a felony. What you *seem* to have here is some psycho who decided to crash my place to pull a wild stunt off."

"We understand you never go to the office on Saturdays."

"Rarely," I said.

"You had an appointment with a person you never met."

"Most of my business is like that."

"Your secretary didn't give you any indication of what the meeting was about," he stated.

"In my business, clients aren't interested in stating their affairs to secretaries. I'm the prime mover."

He stared at me a long moment, then: "The entire charade, it seems, was to set you up to be killed. That it was circumvented is not what we're after. It is why it happened at all. The killer apparently blames you for killing someone."

"And if he went to such lengths to avenge it, then it must have happened?" I waited. Nobody said anything. I added, "Your enigma is a beaut. He left the office alive with an accusation of having already been killed."

"Who is Penta?" Candace Amory asked.

But I was ready for that one too. "Why ask it of a dead man?"

"Because that note was written to be read by a man who wasn't dead yet. He was making sure the victim knew *why* he was dying and *who* was doing the killing. If he thought it was you he was murdering then he knew you would recognize the name before you died."

"Clever thinking, ma'am, very clever. It could be possible, but unfortunately it isn't. Now I want to tell you something right now. If I had any information at all on this matter I would have given it to Pat on the scene last night. We have a fluke going here and I don't know where or how, but damn it, I'm involved now. I'm sure as hell involved. When he put Velda down I was in and I'm going to stay in until that fucking psycho gets nailed to the wall. Sorry about the language, lady, but that's what it's all about."

With a beautifully modulated tone of voice she said, "You'll do nothing of the fucking kind, Mr. Hammer. You stay completely away from this matter or your license will be revoked immediately. Pardon the language, please."

"The ball's in your court," I said sarcastically.

"Yes, I know. And if I were you, I'd reflect a little on the origin of this name Penta. As a matter of fact, I think I'd reflect for no longer than one more day before you have a letter from the Bureau of Licenses." She stood up and looked down at me. "Clear?"

I stood up slowly and she wasn't looking down at me any more. She was tall, but not that tall. "Very clear," I said.

When they walked out of the room Pat let out a short laugh. "She really dumped one on you." He laughed again. "She really doesn't know you very well, does she?"

"Hell, can't she read the papers?" I kicked the chair out and sat down again. "What did your guys find in my office?"

"Nothing."

"Just like that? Nothing?"

"You and Velda laid down most of the prints, some came from the cleaning lady and a couple others seemed to have come from the dead guy. Our killer left smudges, so he was wearing gloves, and not the surgical kind that can transfer prints to surfaces on occasion. The adhesive tape was the kind you buy in any drugstore. He used two full spools of two-inch-wide stuff and took the spools with him."

"They vacuumed, didn't they?"

"And that's tedious lab work. A couple days and we'll see what they picked up."

"Didn't anything turn up on the Penta ID?"

Pat gave me an annoyed scowl and shook his head. "That went out on the wires first thing. Washington, Interpol ... they've all been notified. Trouble is, it's the weekend. Everybody takes off the weekend and some overworked clerk has got everything backed up." He sat back, stretched and said, "What are you planning to tell the Ice Lady?"

"To go piss up a stick."

"Give her Penta instead. She'll love you for it."

"I can do without that. Who is she, anyway?"

Pat got up and poured himself a cup of coffee. He dropped in a couple of Sweet 'n' Lows, sipped it and said, "Somebody the DA has been keeping under wraps. She was the tactician on the two major cases that jumped him into the office last year. Suddenly she wants into field work and you drew her, buddy."

"Great."

"Don't try screwing with her brain. She's a real whiz kid."

"Not if she tried pulling a stupid bluff on me. Who the hell does she think I am, some kid with a new ticket?"

"Believe me," Pat said, she's got something going for her. I'd cover my ass if I were you."

The big clock on the wall read ten twenty-five and I reset my watch. I told Pat I had some things to do and would call in later. He damn well knew what I had in mind and just said so long.

Weekends are the odd times when the regular shift of office maintenance personnel is off and the occasional help comes on. Some are the steadies picking up a few extra bucks, a few are retirees bolstering their pensions and Social Security, and most of them I knew over the years. They were on yesterday and they were on today. The guard in the lobby was an old-timer who let me know the cops had spoken to everyone on the job yesterday and from what he could find out, nobody had anything to offer. Saturday had been a quiet day and, as always, there had been strangers in the building, but that was common and nobody seemed to have stood out from the rest.

I went in the office and Nat Drutman, the building manager, gave me a typed list of the help. "You had some reporters looking for you earlier," he told me.

"Let them in?"

"Temptation almost got me. One guy offered me five bills for a couple of photos."

"What kept you back?"

"Man, the place was still wet from the cleaning. That carpet is going to have to come up."

"They still around?"

"As of an hour ago they were."

"I'll keep my eyes open."

"Why don't you check your office? Those guys'll do anything for a photo."

There were four on the list that could possibly have seen someone going to my office. Unfortunately, the first two hadn't seen anything and like they said, "We wouldn'a told dem cops nothing anyway, Mike. To you we'd say. To them, nuts."

It was the third name that came up with something curious. Her name was Maria Escalante. She changed the sand in the ashtrays at the elevator banks and she was new in the building. I found her dusting the blinds at the far end of the third floor and said, "Miss Escalante?"

She turned, saw me and stiffened. "I have a green card," she said almost defiantly. "I told the others, I have a green card." She reached under her sweater and pulled out a wallet, thumbing its contents. "Look," she told me. "I show it to you." Her Mexican accent was thick.

"That's all right, lady, I believe you."

She tightened up at that. "You are a policeman?"

I rarely ever did it, but I popped my own wallet open to my license. It looked pretty damn official. She shook her head. It wasn't enough.

"Let me see your *pistola*."

That she could understand. I wondered what part of Mexico she came from. I opened my coat and let her see the .45 in the speed rig on my left side.

"*Sí*. I believe. My name is Maria Escalante and I live at . . ."

I waved her off. "I don't need that, Maria."

"I tell the other policemen I don't see nothing. They want to know about the trouble on the floor *ocho* . . . floor eight. I—"

"Maria . . ." I reached out and took her hand and she was shaking. "They scare you about your green card?"

Immediately her mouth tightened and she held back the tears. "One said . . . he could take it . . . that maybe it was no good . . ."

"Is it good?"

"Yes. After the amnesty I get it. I am legal now. I am going to be a US citizen."

"He couldn't take it. He was just trying to shake something out of you, understand?" After a moment she frowned, then bobbed her head. "Where were you yesterday?" I asked.

"From the bottom to floor number . . . five. I did the ashtrays. I ran the sweeper."

"Many people?"

"Some. Mostly it was a day off."

"You know them?"

She nodded again. "They come in, they leave, nobody stay after noontime. Maybe four people."

"Think about ten o'clock. You see anybody then?"

"Who you want me to see?"

I let go her hand. "Beats me. I wish I could answer that."

"One walker is all."

"What's a walker?"

"He comes up the stairs. He walks. The elevator is downstairs a long time, but he walks. He come to floor five and he keeps walking up."

"What time?"

"Just before my break. I go for coffee at ten."

I motioned with my hands, trying to draw some information out of her. "What was he like?"

All I got was a noncommittal shrug.

"Think."

She looked up at the ceiling a few seconds. "He was a big man. He wore a hat." I waited. She shook her head. There was nothing more to add.

"He see you?"

"I did not see his face so he did not see my face," she stated flatly.

"Very big?" I asked her. "Middle-size big?"

She shrugged again. "He wore a coat. Like for the rain."

Like he could put on after a kill to cover up any bloodstains.

"He carry anything?"

Another shrug.

"Did you mention any of this to the other policemen?"

A flash of fear touched her eyes again. "I . . . they made me afraid and I could not think to tell them. Do you think they will . . ."

"Forget it, Maria. You have nothing to worry about at all. Just be a good US citizen, okay?"

I got a little smile then. "*Sí, sí,* very okay," she said.

And now I had a walker. He was big. He wore a raincoat and a hat. There would be a thousand other guys just a few blocks away who could answer that description, but at least it was a start.

There was more that went with the description. He carried some kind of a billy club, but most likely a straight professional blackjack. He had a knife that was honed razor-sharp. It would have to be functional, small enough to carry discreetly, big enough to work efficiently. It could be single- or multi-bladed. I elected for a standard brand-name pocketknife with a four-inch main blade with a possible smaller one opposing. He could have a gun, but guys who prefer steel don't seem to use guns.

That took care of the weaponry.

His personal profile was pretty damn shaggy. He had no compunction about taking out a woman. He felt no revulsion about torturing a victim. He could kill with absolute ease and apparently took a great deal of satisfaction from a grotesque act of murder. He was a deliberate killer and seemed to be acting as an avenger of sorts.

Fear wasn't in his makeup either. He came at me knowing I could put a gun in my hand pretty quickly and would have used it just as fast, but it was his expertise against mine and he was counting on his own.

But he was a dumb son of a bitch because he

*killed the wrong guy. And if he wasn't so dumb he'd
know that and come back to have another try at me.*

And this time I'd have a little avenging going
for me too.

Somebody who was very good had gotten into my
office. A pick had been used on the lock and the
place had been thoroughly searched. The desk
drawers had been pulled open, and only shut to
get at the ones beneath. Both closet doors swung
wide and the filing cabinets had the drawers
completely removed and set on the floor. There
was no ransacking, simply a fast search job for
something big enough to be seen easily.

I put everything back the way it was, not concerned about disturbing prints. Anybody clever
enough to come in with picklocks would have
been enough of a pro to wear plastic gloves.

I had to make five calls before I located Petey
Benson in the Olde English Tavern on Third
Avenue. Ever since he had been on a special
assignment covering a serial killer case in London he had shepherd's pie on Sunday. He was
alone, the remains of his dinner pushed aside,
and he was finishing the paper with a stein of
beer in his hand.

"Now you show up," he said. "Read the paper
yet?"

"Uh-huh."

"Who's sitting on the story? All we got were
official handouts."

"There's a loco loose, Petey. They're playing this one cool."

"Bullshit. What's the story? They said Velda was sapped and there was a killing in your office."

"That's the story. Hell, I came in after it was all over."

"Come on, don't hand me that baloney. A crackpot killing doesn't mean much, but doing it in your office does."

"All I can figure is, some gonzo came in out of the rain with a big mad on at something he thought I did and went after a guy who happened to be in my office at the wrong time. He made a messy job of it and got out without being seen."

"That sounds like a crock."

"It is, but it's the only crock I got."

He gave me a crooked grin and folded his papers up. "So what do you want with me?"

"What's the scoop on Candace Amory?"

"Ah, you have many faces, old boy." He picked up his stein and swirled the beer around. "You want one of these?" Before I could answer he waved to the waiter and motioned for two more steins. "Do you want a personal or a professional opinion?"

"Start with a pro rundown."

"Well educated, intelligent, brainy, intellectual, or is that being redundant?"

"The point's clear."

"She's sharp, mean as a snake, and when it

comes to winning doesn't have any conscience at all. She takes every advantage she can of being a woman and doesn't seem to have chinks in her armor at all. She has powerful friends because she's so damn good at what she does and any political enemies who tried to lean on her didn't know what hit them."

"Great," I said sourly.

"She's got a nice ass, hasn't she?"

"I only saw her from the front."

"That's pretty good too." Petey chuckled. "Why the inquiry?"

"She's coming out in the open," I said. The waiter put the steins down with the handles facing in the wrong direction. I spun the mug around and slopped some of the beer on my sleeve.

Petey took a pull of his beer and wiped the foam from his lip. "Not to be unexpected. That lady has been waiting her chance. I take it she's into this thing with you?"

"She's asking questions."

He took another pull at his drink. "A wonderment," he said. He looked at me across the table, his eyes probing. "We have something big here, I imagine."

"Where did she come from, Petey?"

"Well, nobody does any great research on political appointments of that nature. The DA's office runs a lot of lawyers, plenty of lady lawyers too. But this one was a little special. After she got out of school she spent a year in the FBI, did private legal work in Washington, D.C., then came back to New York. It's easy to see why the DA's office picked up on her."

"She well liked?"

"Beats me, Mike. She probably is, but I don't know how. A lot of the hotshots date her, but she doesn't keep them around very long. She's still not married. Got a nice pad up near the UN." He hoisted the stein and drank the rest of the beer down without a stop. He belched, then said, "You got plans for the lady?"

I did the same thing with my stein but I didn't belch. "Nope," I told him. "It's just better to know what to expect."

That wise old face of his had a knowing expression and he leaned forward and laid his chin in his hands. "Something going down?"

"Something smells funny."

"Like the old days?"

I nodded and my eyes tightened up. "I don't like it, friend. I thought those old days were gone for good."

"Do I get the story?"

"Why not?" I said.

"You watch out for the lovely lady DA. Though I sure would like to see you two tangle, a real kiss 'n' kill situation."

"Thanks a bunch."

"No trouble." I picked up his check when I left. "You can leave the tip," I told him.

3

Burke had wanted Velda to stay quiet as long as possible, so I didn't get to the hospital until eight. We had coffee in the lounge and I asked him how she was progressing.

"She was lucky. You can't imagine how lucky. She was probably on the phone and tossed her hair all to one side while she was talking—"

"A habit she has," I interrupted.

"Anyway, she's awake and sedated."

"Did she say anything to you?"

He popped five spoonfuls of sugar into his coffee and stirred it around. "Sweet tooth," he explained. "No, she said nothing except hello and the usual 'Where am I?' but she's pretty aware of what's going on."

"Can I talk to her?"

"Gently, Mike, gently, and not for long. Nothing exciting."

"How long will she be here?"

"At least two more days. If that was just a simple knockout-type blow she would be home by now, but somebody tried to kill her."

I told him thanks and didn't bother to finish the coffee. I could see why Burke used all that sugar.

Pat had called ahead, and the cop at the door looked at my ID and let me in. The room was in deep gloom, only a small night-light on the wall making it possible to see the outlines of the bed and equipment. When the door snicked shut I picked up the straightbacked chair by the sink, went to the bed and sat down beside her.

Little by little I started to bunch up again, my hands squeezing the rails of the bed. My lips were stretched across my mouth and I wanted to hurt something or tear somebody apart. He should have told me. He never should have let me come in cold and see her like this.

Velda. Beautiful, gorgeous Velda. Those deep brown eyes and that full, full mouth. Shimmering auburn hair that fell in a page-boy around her shoulders.

Now her face was a bloated black-and-blue mask on one side, one eye totally closed under the bulbous swelling, the other a flat slit. Her hair was gone around the bandaged area and her upper lip was twice normal size.

I put my hand over hers and whispered, "Damn it, kitten . . ."

Then her wrist moved and her fingers squeezed mine gently. "Are you . . . all right?" she asked me softly.

"I'm fine, honey, I'm okay. Now don't talk. Just take it easy. All I want is to be here with you. That's enough."

So I just sat there and in a minute she said, "I can . . . listen, Mike. Please tell me . . . what happened."

I played it back to her without building it up at all. I didn't tell her the details of the kill and hinted that it was strictly the work of a nut, but she knew better.

Under my fingers I could feel her pulse. It was steady. Her hand squeezed mine again. "He came in . . . very fast. He had one hand over his face . . . and he was . . . swinging at me . . . with the other. I . . . never saw his face at all." Remembering it hadn't excited her. The pulse rate hadn't changed.

I said, "Okay, honey, that's enough. You're supposed to take it real easy awhile."

But she insisted. "Mike . . ."

"What, kitten?"

"If the police . . . ask questions . . ."

I knew what she was thinking. In her mind she had already put it on a case basis and filed it for immediate activity. There was no way she could be foxed into believing the story of a psycho on the loose. We had been too close too long and now she was reading my mind. She wanted me to have more space to work in, even if she had to be a target herself.

"Play sick," I said.

Until she made a statement, everything was up in the air. She was still alive, so there was a possibility that she could have seen the killer. He couldn't afford any witness at all, but if he tried to erase her he'd be a sitting duck himself. From here on, there would be a solid cover on the hospital room. The killer was going to sweat a little more now.

I thought I saw the good corner of her mouth twitch in a faint smile and again I got the small finger squeeze. "Be careful," she said. Her voice was barely audible and she was slipping back into a sleep once more. "I want ... you back."

Her fingers loosened and her hand slipped out of mine. She didn't hear me when I said, "I want you back too, baby."

Outside the door the cop said, "How is she?"

"Making it." He was a young cop, this one. He still had that determined look. He had the freshness of youth, but his eyes told me he had seen plenty of street work since he left the academy. "Did Captain Chambers tell you what this was about?" I asked.

"Only that it was heavy. The rest I got through the grapevine."

"It's going to get rougher," I said. "Don't play down what you're doing."

He grinned at me. "Don't worry, Mike, I'm not jaded yet."

"Way to go, kiddo."

"By the way . . ."

"What's that?"

"How come you never locked into the department?"

"King Arthur wouldn't let me go."

"That's right," he laughed. "I forgot, you're the Black Knight."

"Take care of my girl in there, will you?"

His face suddenly went serious. "You got it, Mike."

Downstairs another shift was coming on, fresh faces in white uniforms replacing the worn-out platoon that had gone through a rough offensive on the day watch. The interns looked too young to be doctors, but they already had the wear and tear of the profession etched into them. One had almost made it to the door when the hidden PA speaker brought him up short, and with an expression of total fatigue, he shrugged and went back inside.

I cut around the little groups and pushed my way through the outside door. The rain had stopped, but the night was clammy, muting the street sounds and diffusing the lights of the buildings. Nights like this stunk. There were no in-coming taxis and it was a two-block walk to where they might cruise by. There was no other choice, so I went down the steps to the street. Behind me two interns were debating waiting for a nurse who had a car, then decided they were too tired to wait and followed me, taking the other side of the street.

At night this area was solid bumper-to-bumper parked cars, wedged so tightly together you wanted to see how they came unstuck in the morning. A smart one had a two-foot space in front of him with his wheels cranked hard away from the curb so he couldn't be pushed up, and I walked right past it like a Jersey tourist before I knew it didn't fit and the slight metallic creak of a door was wrong and everything exploded at once.

Ducking and twisting was automatic and some-thing whispered by over my head. Then a pair of bodies were on me, fists smashing at my kidneys and bouncing off my neck. I rammed my elbow back and felt teeth go under it and the back of my head mashed the guy's nose who was holding me. I was off balance and before I could use my feet another flying pair of arms nailed my legs together in a crude tackle and we all hit the pavement with me on the bottom. My .45 was still tight in the shoulder holster and I felt a hand going under my coat and yanking it clear.

It wasn't a mugging. I felt the needle go into

my hip and within seconds the drowsiness started. Somebody was cursing and spitting blood behind me, and when I had no strength left the restraining arms fell away and I heard a voice saying he wanted to kick my brains out for breaking his nose.

It wasn't dream time. There were faraway sounds and feelings of being in motion. I could hear voices, but didn't know what they were saying. And it was black. I felt tired and wanted to sleep, but I was in a limbo all alone.

Time itself had no meaning. Its passage I could record by the throbbing where my body hurt, but no other way. So I just let it all happen, thinking of what a damned sucker I had been for letting myself get trapped. I said, "Shit," and my ears heard it and I let my eyes slide open and lifted my head up.

Somebody said, "He's awake."

There was barely any light and it came from a small open bulb thirty feet away. I was tied to a chair, my arms and legs snug to it and two turns of rope holding me tight against the back. There was no sense wasting any strength thrashing around. Pros had done this job and I could barely make out the form of one of them in front of me, his face an indistinguishable pale orb. There was another behind me and he wasn't breathing right. He kept swearing under his breath and spitting on the floor.

A hand came out of the darkness and tilted my

head back. The beam of a small flashlight swept across my eyes and the voice said, "It's all worn off. He's wide awake." It was an accented voice, but nothing I could place.

The other one sounded like he had a bad cold, his words whispery deep with a rasp to it. He moved in closer, but I still couldn't make out his face. "Tell us about Penta," he said.

Sometimes you have to mouth off. I told him, "Up yours."

His hand came around and there was no way I could move. It was a flat-handed slap with a hell of a lot of meat behind it and I could taste blood in my mouth.

"One more time, Hammer."

"Asshole," I said.

The hand got me again, harder than before. My ear was ringing so badly I hardly heard the other voice say, "Knock if off. We haven't got time for this."

"You just let me . . ."

"Damn it, you're not playing with some patsy. He's been through the rough stuff before. Give him the sodium Pentothal."

I thought now somebody would come in close enough for me to get a good look at them, but an oily smelling towel was tossed over my head, then somebody pulled my sleeve back. I felt the cold touch of an alcohol swab, then a needle went into my forearm.

Again, reality drifted away. It took all my defenses with it and I could hear and speak and even see light through the worn towel. A little part of my brain told me if I fought real hard I could lie right through the truth serum, but then, why bother lying when telling the truth was so much fun?

"Who is Penta?"

"I don't know."

"Where is Penta now?"

"I don't know."

"When did you meet Penta?"

"I never met Penta."

"Who is Penta?"

"I don't know."

The first voice said, "Let's increase the dosage." I felt the needle again. There was another long pause before the questions started. I gave them the same answers. It was almost a pleasure to be able to do it.

Another needle, and this time they waited almost too long. The sleep was coming on me.

The voice said, "I am Penta."

Only my brain made an idiotic grin. If I said he wasn't, it would mean I knew Penta.

My tongue said, "Good for you."

"Do you work for Penta?"

They were trying it again.

"I work . . . by myself." The words didn't come out easily at all.

The raspy one said, "He's going."

"Well, that's it," his partner told him.

"You think he was faking it?"

"I don't know how he could."

Sounds were too faint now to register and I felt myself being jostled around, then the sleep came and the strange, fuzzy chemical dreams that had no direction or substance, shooting off into one area after another like a firefight pattern of tracer bullets gone wild.

Awakening was in slow motion, one part at a time. I stayed immobile until I had things back in focus again, trying to remember what had preceded the odd stupor I was in. Then the mental door unlatched and it was all there, not totally clear, but discernible enough.

The ropes holding me in the chair had been loosened, with just enough tension there to keep me from falling off the chair. I shook them loose, then leaned forward and stood up. I was shaky, so I didn't move for a minute.

No drugs were lousing me up now and I could see better in the light from that dull bulb than I could before. I was in some kind of a garage, the oil and grease smell thick, dull forms of heavy machinery on either side of me. On the floor, in front of my feet, was my hat. Next to it was my .45.

Bending down was easy. Getting back up wasn't. I put the .45 back in the holster and straightened out my hat.

No, that wasn't a mugging. That was as far away from a mugging as you could get. I still had my money in my wallet and when I looked at my watch it read four fifteen.

A wide sliding door was on the other side of the light with a normal door built into it. I twisted the lock, pulled on the knob and went out to the street. A sign over the door read SMILEY'S AUTO-MOTIVE in old hand-painted letters. I walked to the corner slowly, saw where I was, then crossed the street and went another long block to where the lights were, waited a good five minutes, then flagged down a taxi.

The driver's eyes met mine in the rearview mirror. "You okay, mac?"

I nodded. "Yeah, just been one of those nights." I gave him my address and closed my eyes.

Pat looked at me with total disgust and jammed his hands in his pockets. "Mike, what kind of clown crap you call this? You let ten hours go by before you give me the story of what happened. You think we wouldn't have responded right away?"

"They were pros."

"Pros can leave marks behind," he reminded me.

"What did you find?"

"Okay, nothing of importance. The chair, ropes. Somebody spit blood on the floor. Type O positive."

"And that's half the population," I said. "At least there's somebody with some teeth out of whack and another dude with a busted nose probably sporting a pair of beautiful black eyes right now. You get anything more from the owner?"

"Zilch, that's what. Smiley's place has been in that spot for over twenty years. During the slow season he shuts down and heads for the tracks. Playing the ponies is his one vice."

"That's not a great area to leave a business alone, buddy."

"What's he got to steal? A couple of hydraulic presses for straightening car frames? What're you getting at anyway?"

"The guys who had me knew the place would be empty."

"Hell, there were two other places down the street that were empty too." He stopped and breathed in deeply. "Maybe we'll get lucky and find a broken nose or de-toothed slob who has grease marks on his shoe soles we can identify."

"Don't bother. They would have thought of that too."

"Why didn't you answer your phone?"

"Because I was beat. There wasn't one damn thing I could have done."

"When those interns called 911 we had you ID'd in fifteen minutes. Every car in the city was scrounging around looking for you."

"How about the car they threw me into?"

"A black Mercedes. Late model and nobody got the number. One intern said the right rear taillight was out. So far, we haven't located it."

"So what are you all pissed off about?" I asked him. "I'm here, nothing's happened and we know somebody else is looking for the Penta character too."

Pat took another of those comforting deep breaths, quieted down and then told me, "We have all the information on the late Anthony DiCica."

"Oh?"

"Forget those minor counts in New York. DiCica turns out to have been an enforcer for the New York mob. He was a suspect in four homicides, never got tapped for any of them and gained a reputation of being a pretty efficient workman."

"Then how'd he get to be a delivery man?"

"Simple. Somebody cracked his skull open in a street brawl and he came all unraveled. He was in a hospital seven months and left with severely impaired mental faculties."

"Who sponsored him?"

"Nobody took him in. He remembered very little of his past, but he could handle uncomplicated things. He had been working with that printer you used for over a year. The hospital had no choice except to release him."

"What's the tag line, Pat?"

"He could have made enemies. Somebody saw him and came after him."

"In my office?"

"Anybody with a hate big enough to take him apart like that wouldn't be rational about it. He'd take him when and where he could and your office was it. He spotted him, followed him, then went in after him. If your unknown client did show up afterward all the activity scared him off."

For a minute I thought about it. There was still the "walker" Maria Escalante had seen, but for now I was keeping that to myself. I said, "Why the hell was I abducted then, Pat? Nobody wanted me. They wanted Penta."

A detective came in and handed Pat a thick folder and left. Pat flopped it open, scowled, then closed the office door, sealing out the confusion on the other side. "Mike, you remember Ray Wilson?"

"Sure. The old intelligence guy?"

"He's had Penta on the computers with Washington for two days. Usually we get some sort of a reply in a short, reasonable time. With Penta it's all delays and referrals to other agencies."

"What's that supposed to mean?"

"Probably nothing," Pat said. "Ray seems to think that when Penta was mentioned a flag went up somewhere down the line. When that happens we're into something pretty damn heavy."

I let out a laugh. "And I can see what will drop on you if they know we have such great heart-to-heart talks." I looked around. "This place bugged?"

He looked startled a second, then grinned. "Go

screw yourself, pal. You're *my* pigeon and I'm running you."

"Good story," I said. "Stick to it." I looked at my watch. It was almost four o'clock. "When's the next briefing?"

"Like now," Pat said. "Let's go."

This time the Ice Lady wore a cool blue sheath of a fabric that seemed to caress her whenever she moved. She knew what it did and every motion was beautifully orchestrated for her audience. Their response was just as carefully calculated, as though they were totally ignorant of this vibrant woman who was one of them too. They saw us come in, but only stopped talking when we were close enough to hear what they were saying.

Pat motioned to the table. "Shall we sit down?"

I didn't bother with the chair bit this time. I took a seat across from Jerome Coleman and when he was ready, he nodded to the man next to him and said, "This is Frank Carmody and his assistant, Phillip Smith, both of the Federal Bureau of Investigation. On my right is Mr. Bennett Bradley, representing the State Department, and his special assistant from the CIA, Mr. Lewis Ferguson."

It's funny how cops look like cops. When they're federal they seem to dress alike, groom themselves identically and use the same body language. There were slight differences in the color and pattern of their suits, but not much. They were all in their early forties and probably had the same barber who gave proper haircuts and shaved close.

At least Bradley, the guy from State, was different. His suit was a light gray, his tie was red and he wore a mustache, which was more hair than he had on his head. Like Yul Brynner's, it was shaved off on the back of his skull for convenience. But he was still State, bore the bureaucratic attitude of tired integrity and seemed anxious to get on with the meeting.

Pat said, "I'm Captain Chambers and this is Michael Hammer. I believe you want to ask him some questions."

I held up my hand before they could talk. "This is a strange interagency relationship here. Cooperation between the FBI and CIA is pretty damn rare. Not to mention State. Do I need a lawyer here?"

The Ice Lady said, "You are not in jeopardy, Mr. Hammer."

"My licenses are intact, I presume."

"For now." There was no inflection in her voice at all.

I gestured with my hand and sat back.

Carmody spoke up first. "We want to know about Penta, Mr. Hammer."

"So does everybody else," I told him.

"Yes. We've all read the statement you gave Captain Chambers. The witnesses at the hospital saw the assailants, saw you abducted, and we know what you have said."

"What's your point?"

It was Bennett Bradley from the State Department who broke in. "Mr. Hammer . . . when your name came up in this matter I remembered having heard it before. After an inquiry or two I opened a file that made interesting reading."

Pat grunted and said, "Everything he does is interesting."

Bradley simply ignored him and said, "You testified at a trial as to the possible inaccuracy of the polygraph test. In fact, you gave a demonstration using an authorized operator of the device and succeeded in lying without being detected."

"There were two others who did the same thing, Mr. Bradley. If you know how to do it there's no trick to it at all."

"The State lost that case, I might add."

"So be it," I said. "What's that got to do with now?"

"Could you possibly do it under sodium Pentothal?"

They were playing with me now and I was getting ticked off. "I suppose there could be a trick to that too."

All of them watched me, waiting.

I said, "Why are you so interested in nailing this loony?"

It was Lewis Ferguson who looked to Pat for

confirmation and when Pat nodded slightly, he said, "This one . . . this Penta murdered one of our men. You seem to have enough . . . familiarization with police departments to understand how we feel about this."

"I know how the cops feel about it."

"We're no different."

"Cops don't have the State Department backing them up," I said.

Bradley gave me an enigmatic smile. Those State guys had a thing with them that made me want to belt them right in the mouth. "The agent who was killed was carrying some very valuable information. If he gave it up before he died, the security of the United States could be compromised."

"Oh, for Pete's sake, I've heard that 'compromised' line a million times. What the hell can one man carry that could destroy us? You know damn well nobody can afford to start tossing nukes around and live to brag about it, so how the hell do we get compromised?"

"I'm not referring to the big nations, Mr. Hammer. Some of the Third World countries have nuclear capabilities nobody likes to speak about. They may not have the same moral attitudes we have."

"So why kill your agent?"

"Because he knew which country was planning to let the first bird fly. He was about to deliver that information."

"Damn," I said, "here I was thinking about how altruistic you were about your agent getting killed. Things are starting to blossom out."

"Mr. Hammer," Ferguson said. "Did you lie to your abductors about Penta?"

I shrugged. It was better than words. Finally I told them, "I don't know. I was under the influence of drugs."

They were very polite and thanked me. The Ice Lady looked at me and her eyes were as cool as her dress. She turned just a little bit and the fold of her neckline opened enough to show the fullness of her breasts, snowy white against icy blue. I didn't try to hide my appreciation, and let her see the edges of my teeth under a smile.

Pat and I looked at each other in the empty room and he said, "Want to go have coffee?"

"Sure. Think we can get Ray Wilson to go with us?"

"He's always glad to go anywhere." He pushed back his chair. "What do you want him for, anyway?"

I said, "You reminded me that he was in the intelligence unit."

"Fourteen years' worth."

"Didn't he head up the operation when Qaddafi threatened personal attacks on Reagan?"

"He headed up the New York command post. Incidentally, he's our liaison with some international counterparts." He frowned, looking at me quizzically. "Why?"

"Maybe he can straighten out a few things for me."

"Beautiful. Never say New York's Finest doesn't do its damnedest to keep the public happy."

"Come on, pal, I pay my taxes," I said.

"Don't forget your license fees."

"Never," I grinned. "Now, do we go downstairs together or one at a time?"

Pat shook his head at me. "After all these years, this department has given up on you and me."

"Not the DA's office, though."

"Ah, them," Pat said. "They come and go with the elections. Just don't underplay Candace Amory, buddy."

Musingly, I said, "The Ice Lady."

"Yeah, her."

"She's going to supper with me," I told him.

"Bullshit." He seemed startled. "When did this happen?"

"As soon as I ask her, kiddo."

Ray Wilson was already at a table when we got to the deli, a half-eaten pastrami sandwich and an empty coffee cup in front of him. "Couldn't wait for you guys," he explained. "Want coffee?" We both nodded and he held up two fingers. Before we were in the booth the waiter had the coffee down. The old cop went back to his sandwich, had another bite and added, "Nobody ever asks me out for anything unless they want something."

"How about women?" I suggested.

"Boy oh boy, do *they* want something. My apartment, my salary, my pension."

"Just because you're good-looking?"

"Man," he leered, "I may not be a beauty, but I sure got something that is. Well trained. Knows all the tricks. But that's not what you want to know about. So what's up?"

"Mike's been thinking," Pat said.

He nodded and waited.

I said, "You know about me being mugged. I mean, *classically* mugged?"

"Pat told me," he said casually.

"Two of them questioned me about Penta. Their voices were accented, but at the time I was pretty cloudy from the shot they had given me and didn't try to place the inflections. Every time I think back now I seem to come to one conclusion. Those accents were faked."

"Well?"

My coffee was too hot to drink, so I sipped at it. "What's your opinion on Penta?"

Wilson gave Pat another of those looks and Pat gave him the "go ahead" sign with his hands. He said to me, "I assume you're asking me if the guys who grabbed you were from some government agency?"

"You got it."

"Why?"

"Their method, their attitude. All that was pretty well structured."

"Hell, Mike, even a bunch of punks could do that.

"Would punks want Penta?"

Pat held up his hand and interrupted. "Suppose as a mob hit man, DiCica thought he had killed Penta and didn't. That still leaves him open to be knocked off."

"Where does that put me then?" I asked Pat.

"In the middle, pal, right in the frigging middle. If you know *anything* about Penta, they wanted to know about it."

"Then why did they leave my gun right there on the floor? No punk is going to walk away from a piece like that."

Wilson let out a derisive laugh. "With the pieces we get in off the street, nobody would want an antique .45 like yours. Nowadays the hoods opt for Uzis, .357 Magnums and anything untraceable. A registered piece like your Colt could mean trouble."

"Right," I agreed. "But if they *did* come from some agency everything would still fit."

"True." Wilson finished his sandwich, wiped his hands on a napkin and lit up a butt. "All you wanted was my opinion?"

"That's all."

"Okay, they weren't hoods. They had some intelligence going for them. They knew about the hospital, they had the car preparked, ready for a quick getaway. Sodium Pentothal or a quick-acting tranquilizer could be easy to get, but using

Smiley's garage meant plenty of preknowledge. One other thing, after you damaged two of their guys nobody bothered to lay anything on you. That's a real professional attitude."

He stopped, took a long drag on his butt and let the smoke drift toward the ceiling, watching it laze its way upward. "So they were government personnel?"

"I didn't say which government. Or whose," he replied easily. "Besides, all you wanted was an opinion."

"There were FBI and CIA troops probing for more of the same an hour ago."

"Carmody and Ferguson," he stated.

"Those are the ones."

"Old spooks. I know them. Good guys but dull. They were real busy during the Black Panther days. Later Ferguson spent a lot of time overseas helping smooth over some of the blunders we made."

"You're real current, Ray."

He winked at Pat. "Interdepartmental cooperation, they call it."

Now I took my time about polishing off my coffee. When it was gone I put it down slowly. Little things were beginning to show. I said, "Where does Bradley come into it?"

"He's a State Department troubleshooter."

"On what level?" I asked him.

"That I don't know. He spent the last six

months in England and was rotated back here about three weeks ago."

Someplace there had to be a connection. "Penta's beginning to have an international flavor."

"Not necessarily," Wilson told me. "State might be into this just to protect one of their own sources. Washington gets pretty damn touchy about the contacts they have running for them."

"Like Pat runs me?"

Wilson grunted something unintelligible. "Yeah."

"So who the hell is Penta?" I asked.

"And why did you kill him?" Pat said. When I gave him a nasty look he added, "That damn note meant something, Mike."

"Not if it was DiCica he was really after. In that case you guys have a plain old murder and not some kind of conspiracy." I got up to leave and tossed a buck down for my coffee.

"Somehow," Pat insisted, "that note is important. Just how do you explain him saying 'You die for killing me'?"

"Easy," I said.

They both looked up at me.

"Somebody gave him AIDS."

Pat's eyes got hard and I waved him off before he could say anything. "Wasn't me, buddy," I said.

I thought the little guy in the oddball suit who shuffled up to me was another panhandler. When I closed the cab door he peered at me, a grin twisting his mouth, and said, "Remember me? I'm Ambrose."

"Ambrose who?"

"How many people with a name like that you know? From Charlie the Greek's place, man."

Then I remembered him behind a mop getting the spilled beer off the floors. They called him Ambie then.

He said, "Charlie says for you to give him a call."

"Why?"

"Beats me, man. He just told me to tell you that. And the sooner the better. It's important."

I told him okay, handed him two bucks and watched him scuttle away. When I got upstairs I dug out the old phone book, looked up the Greek's place and called Charlie. His raspy voice started chewing me out for not stopping by the past six months and when he got finished he said, "There's a gent that wants to meet with you, Mike."

Charlie was an old-fashioned guy. When he said "gent" it was with capital quote marks around it, printed in red. Any "gent" would be somebody in the chain of command that led into the strange avenues of what they deny is organized crime. He wasn't connected; he was simply a useful tool in the underworld apparatus.

"He got a name, Charlie?"

"Sure, I guess. But I don't know it."

"What's the deal?"

"Like tonight. Can you make it down here tonight?"

"You know what time it is?"

"Since when are you a day person?"

"He there now?"

"I got a number to call. He can be here in an hour."

I looked at my watch. "Okay, but make it two. You think I ought to have some backup?"

"Naw. This guy's clean."

"Tell him to sit at the bar."

"You got it, Mike."

The Greek's place was just a run-down old saloon in a neighborhood that was going under the wrecker's ball little by little. Half the places had been abandoned, but Charlie's joint was near the corner, got a regular trade and a lot of daytime transients. From four to seven every evening the gay crowd took over like a swing shift, then left abruptly and everything went back to sloppy normalcy.

A pair of old biddies were sipping beer at the end of the bar and right in the center was a middle-aged portly guy in a dark suit having a highball. His eyes picked me up in the back bar mirror when I came in and we didn't have to be introduced. He waved Charlie over. I said, "Canadian Club and ginger," then we picked up the drinks and went to a table across the room.

"Appreciate your coming," he said.

"No trouble. What's happening?"

"There are some people interested in Tony DiCica's death."

"Pretty messy subject. You know what happened to him?"

He bobbed his head. "Tough."

"Yeah. He sure as hell messed up my office. But that's not what you want to know."

He stared around the room, then sipped at his drink. "You and that police officer checked out his apartment."

"Right."

"Did you find anything?"

"There was a loaded clip from an automatic, but no gun. The only thing he had was an old toolbox."

"You're coming at me fast and easy, buddy."

"Negative answers are easy to give."

"That place really get shaken down?"

"We didn't take it apart." I pushed my drink aside. I still hadn't tasted it. "What should we have found?"

He gave me a long, steady look, then showed a little smile. "You would have known."

Now I tasted my drink. Charlie had given me a double charge and barely taste it was all I did. The guy opposite was watching me curiously, not quite knowing how to steer the conversation. Finally I said, "Let's get something squared away here. You guys don't give a shit who knocked off DiCica, do you?"

"Couldn't care less."

"Don't hand me that," I told him. "You mean *unless* he got from Tony what you wanted."

After thinking about it he acknowledged the point. "Something like that."

I said, "You know, I don't give a rat's ass what Tony had. The guy who took him out thought he was me, and *I* give a shit who did the killing."

"Some people aren't going to look at it that way," he told me. "Until they're absolutely satisfied, you're going to have a problem."

"There's one hell of a hole in your presentation, fella," I said. "Tony's been running loose a long time. If he had something, why didn't they get it from him when he was alive?"

"You know about Tony's history?"

"I know."

"If you guess the answer I'll tell you if it's right."

Hell, there could only be one answer. I said, "Tony had something he could hang somebody with." The guy kept watching me. "He had permanent amnesia after getting his head bashed in and didn't remember having it or putting it somewhere." The eyes were still on mine. The storyline started to open up now. "Just lately he said or did something that might indicate a sudden return of memory." The eyes narrowed and I knew I had it.

When he put his drink away in two quick swallows, he rolled the empty glass in his fingers a moment. "It came in the day he was killed. A week before he suddenly recognized somebody *they* kept close to him and called him by his right name."

"Then he relapsed back into the amnesia again?"

"Nobody knows that."

"Don't tell me they never checked his apartment before."

"Twice. Didn't find a damn thing. If they had splintered the place he might have panicked. After all, he was living in a whole new world. If he stayed that way and the stuff stayed with him everything would've been okay. But he came out of it."

Now I was beginning to see what he was getting at. "And you think somebody else was watching him too, waiting for him to shake off the amnesia."

He just looked at me, not saying a word.

"Where do I come in?" I asked him.

"Mike, you got a big reputation, you know that?"

"So?"

"You have your fingers in all kinds of shit. You move with the clean guys and you go with the dirty ones just as easy. Nobody likes to mess with you because you've blown a few asses off with that cannon of yours and you got buddies up in Badgeville where it counts. So you'd be just the kind of guy Tony DiCica would run to with a story that would keep his head on his shoulders."

"Crazy," I said.

"Not really. He'd been to your office three times before."

"Business with the printer. My secretary took care of it."

"You say. He could have been discussing *his* business."

"Wrong," I stated.

"Can you prove otherwise?"

I thought a second. "No."

"The day he was killed he had come in to arrange something with you. Before you got there somebody else showed up and did the job, expecting to walk away with the information. He didn't have it on him, but he sure would have talked when he was getting his fingers whacked off."

This thing was really coming back at me. "Okay, what's my part?"

"He is your client, Mr. Hammer. He has told you all in return for an escape route you are to furnish."

"That's a lot of bullshit, you know."

A gesture of his hands meant it didn't make any difference. "You see, as far as certain people are concerned, you are in until they say you're out. The information Tony had can be worth a lot of money and can cause a lot of killing. One way or another, they expect to get it back."

"What happens if the cops get it first?"

"Nobody really expects that to happen," he

said. He pulled his cuff back and looked at his watch. "If the killer didn't get the info from Tony he'll be thinking the same way the others are . . . that you have it or know where it is."

I took one more sip of my drink and stood up. "I guess everybody wants me dead."

"At least *certain* people are giving you a few days of grace to make a decision."

I could feel my lips pulling back in controlled anger and knew it wasn't a nice grin at all. I pulled the .45 out, watched his eyes go blank until I flipped out the clip and fingered a shell loose. I handed it to him. "Give them that," I said.

"What's this supposed to mean?"

"They'll know," I told him.

I've often wondered how Petey Benson got his information. The phone was his friend and the taxis were his ally. He seemed to know nobody, yet knew everybody. Twice in recent years his inside stories blew two administrations out of office and his penetration into a Wall Street operation almost wrecked a bank. Crime wasn't his bag, but devious causes were. Breaking down the intricate machinations of the power jockeys brought a glow to his face.

We met in front of the Plaza Hotel, then ducked inside to the bar. At this time there were only two others at the far end, immersed in their own business. Petey slid an envelope to me and I pulled out two sheets of handwritten notes and a photostat.

Petey asked me, "Want a drink?"

I wanted to read the notes, but said, "CC and ginger."

What he had scribbled were highlights of Candace Amory's background. Her family was one of those deadly kind that dropped a smoldering genius into the political arena every other generation, spewing out minor luminaries along the way. None of the Amorys ever really made the big time because they were smart enough to stay where the power base could be manipulated. Within her own family Candace Amory was a wild hair up everybody's ass, but seemingly controllable.

It was the photostat that laid it all out. Petey had finished his drink, so I pushed mine over to him. "Where did you get this?" I asked him.

"Trade secret."

What I had was an essay the Ice Lady had written. It was a statement of fact so direct, so concisely put together that I knew this was an exact timetable that Miss Amory was going to adhere to and fulfill. The young Candace was promising that she would be the district attorney of New York City, thence to the governorship of the state and from there to the presidency of the United States.

If she hadn't already made it into the DA's office and already insinuated herself into a first-class, spectacular news story, I would have said

it was just the drivel the young and inexperi-
enced enjoy fantasizing about.

But this was real.

"Clue me, Petey. Things like this just don't
lay around. Where did you dig it up?"

"Buy me another drink."

I bought him another drink.

"You haven't figured it out yet?"

"No. I'm a dumb detective."

"Go to college, Mike?"

"Sure I did, why?"

"They make you do an essay on yourself as
part of your admittance application?"

"Damn," I said. "That was pretty sharp, buddy.
And they just handed this over to you?"

Across his fresh drink he said, "No, I stole it.
You see, those are things I know how to do. Help
any?"

"It gives me an edge," I told him.

"You'll need more than that if you tangle
assholes with that lady."

"Well, no guts, no glory," I said. I reached in
my pocket and dug out some change. "I suppose
you know her phone number?"

He said sure and gave it to me, reminding me
that it was unlisted. So much for privacy. "What're
you calling her for?"

"I'm going to ask her out to supper."

"Hell, man, it's already suppertime. Women
don't buy *that* kind of action."

"This one might," I said.

I went out to a pay phone and called the Ice Lady. She said she had nothing better to do and would meet me at the Four Seasons. I told her she would meet me at the Pub on Fifty-seventh Street since I was buying. She knew better than to argue. I had a date.

Petey said, "Well?"

I glanced at my watch. "I'll see her in half an hour."

His mouth dropped open. "How did you *manage* that?"

"To paraphrase you, old buddy," I told him, "that is one of the things *I* know how to do."

What I didn't tell him was that I knew she'd been sitting there waiting for me to call ever since she put on that show with her titties.

The Irishman who ran the Pub gave me a big hello, reserved a table for me in back and set up a Miller Lite on the bar while I waited. I was early because I knew she'd be early. Anyone who wanted the presidency *had* to be early.

She smiled coming in the door and I said, "Good evening, Miss Amory."

"Hello, Mr. Hammer. Am I in time?"

"Right on the button. Want a drink at the bar or shall we go back to the table?"

"Oh, let's go to the table. It's been a long day. I'd rather sit down."

I waved toward the rear and let her follow the waiter. The Pub had good Irish class, great corned beef and typical New York customers. It wasn't upper crust and the elite choose other places to see or be seen, and from her surreptitious motions I knew Candace Amory was putting it in a niche of its own, adding another check mark on my character sheet.

When we sat down I said, "It's a good address."

Puzzled, she looked at me, a cigarette halfway to her lips. "What?"

"Nothing." I pointed to the butt between her fingers. "Why do you smoke?"

"Habit I suppose." Again she seemed puzzled.

"A mouth like yours doesn't need a cigarette in it."

Her tongue flicked out and wet her lips. "Oh? What does it need, Mr. Hammer?"

I gave her a little smile and her face got red. I got her off the hook nice and easy. "How about a hot corned beef sandwich?"

For a minute there some of the frost had melted on the Ice Lady, but the confusion only lasted a few moments. At least the first points were mine. She put the cigarette down.

A lot of things can get said across a dinner table. The mere fact of eating gives you time to think, to plan, to probe. We each had our own reasons for being there and all the weapons were out in the open.

The lady was coolly conscious of the way her dress accentuated the curve of her bosom, showing you just so much, yet letting you know there was so much more to be seen. When she'd walked to the table, shrugging the coat off her shoulders, she knew that eyes were watching her, drinking up her catlike grace, taking in sharp breaths at the sensuous rhythm of her walk. Now I had all her weaponry concentrated on me and I was glad I had enough years on me to tell me not to get blindsided like an amateur.

"Tell me, Mr. Hammer . . ."

"Mike."

"Then you may call me Candace."

"Never Candy?"

"No, never. And I am Candace only socially."

"Wouldn't be proper at a board meeting?"

She smiled. "Nor in a courtroom."

"Now what did you want me to tell you?" I asked.

"What your motives are in asking me for supper."

I took another bite of the corned beef. "To get you to open up and let me in on what's happening. Our Penta guy is getting some pretty high-level attention."

"Deservedly so."

"Bradley never mentioned the name of the agent who was murdered."

"Naturally."

"Do you know?"

She shook her head. "Nor do I want to. Dead men are . . . dead. The live ones can be made to talk and put on a witness stand. We are looking for a multiple killer now, a torture murderer

who has to be stopped before he gets to somebody else."

"And that's what you really wanted to know in
the beginning, wasn't it, Candace?"

This time her expression went through a vari-
ety of phases before it steadied into a defiant
stare. "Tell me," she said deliberately.

"How come I'm not scared to death to be out
alone knowing Penta wanted me? *If* I was the
one he wanted."

"You amaze me, Mike. Why aren't you?"

"All of a sudden I'm on my toes. I don't feel
like being mugged again. I don't like being a
target, either, so the first slob who goes to do a
heavy on me is going to get a slug up his kiester.
Or wherever."

"Wherever sounds better." This time she got
into her sandwich.

"Tell me something, Candace, aren't you spooked
about the way all this is being handled?" She
kept eating, waiting for an explanation. "Everybody is talking to me, inviting me in for open
conferences, ostensibly giving me classified information . . . everything that's in direct viola-
tion of law-enforcement practices."

"Not necessarily. Witnesses can be treated . . . in
a friendly fashion."

"Again, pardon the language, bullshit. You damn
well know that I'm not anything so far. I'm an
innocent bystander in a murder, a victim in a
mugging and a suspect of an indefinable sort at

this point. But I'm something else too, lady. I'm a guy with a reputation that has to hold the line. I'm a damn headhunter and I get the feeling every one of you are standing by waiting to see who makes the first move and hoping I can simplify your case with a .45 in Penta's nose."

She took a ladylike nibble at her sandwich. "Very forcefully said."

"So why the heavy hitters from the agencies?"

Once again she timed it nicely, finishing her coffee before she made her decision. "My friend Jerome Coleman was formerly with the FBI."

I took a wild shot. "He was one of your instructors at the academy in Norfolk, wasn't he?" The guess was right and caught her completely off guard.

"Why ... yes." Her eyes were asking me a question.

"Just something I picked up," I said. Her association with the FBI would be public information, but not her friendship with Coleman. "Go on."

"He was in my office when we got news of the murder in your office. The name Penta touched something in his memory and he called Frank Carmody. That's when the federal agencies came into the picture. Penta was wanted for the murder of their man overseas."

"They must have a description of him," I suggested.

"Not an iota. No prints, no photos, nothing."

"Where did all this happen?"

"England. Somewhere in England. Outside Manchester, I think."

"Yet they know his name."

"Yes. I don't know how."

I was getting some ideas, but they would take time to look into. Now I had to let her have her turn. I said, "What can I do for you?"

She looked down at the small diamond-studded watch on her wrist. "Take me home, for one thing. We can talk on the way."

I paid the bill and walked her out of the place, enjoying the envious looks I got. This time her walk was more sedate, but she couldn't hide the contours of her body. A cab was at the curb and we got in and she gave the driver her address. We were almost there when I said to her, "You haven't answered my question yet, Candace."

"I've been told you're very aggressive," she started.

"Sure, I'm in a tough business."

"Then tell me ... what do you plan on doing about this ... matter?"

The lady asked some dramatic questions, all right. The cab pulled up outside her apartment, a uniformed doorman ran up, opened the door and we got out. He said good evening to Candace, barely nodded to me, then seemed to recognize me and nodded again, annoyed because he didn't remember my name.

"Would you care to come up for a drink?"

No way I'd spoil her plan of attack. I said yes,

went inside, took the elevator up to the twelfth floor and did the bit of opening the door for her with her own keys.

Miss Candace Amory lived like the princess she was. The place was magazine-picture perfect, a miniature New York castle that unlimited money could buy. The damned place even looked comfortable. I think the music started automatically when we walked in, something low and sultry and classical. It was nearly nine thirty and I wondered when Ravel's *Bolero* would come on.

"What are you smiling about?"

"Appreciating your house."

"Is it suitably seductive?"

"Fits you well," I said.

She laughed, said, "I suppose now I should go in and put on something more comfortable. Is that my line?"

"Doesn't matter. I can handle buttons and snaps."

"Touché. Make us a drink while I call my office."

I went to the bar and built a pair of highballs. I put them on the coffee table and took a seat in the overstuffed chair across from the matching sofa. I wondered how she would handle this one.

She listened to her messages, wrote down some notes, then dialed again. The person she spoke to was the district attorney. She told him she'd be home all night, then came over, picked up her drink and eased herself down on the sofa. "Afraid of me?"

"Nope." I lifted my glass in a toast. "Cheers."

"Cheers," she said. "Once more. What are *your* plans?"

"Legally," I told her, "I have no position at all. I can contribute knowledge and information to the police department and associated agencies, but I stay hands-off on the case itself."

"I didn't ask you about legalities."

My drink tasted good. Smooth. I gave her a little shrug. "I'm a victim seeking redress."

"Bullshit to you too," she said.

A grin started slowly, tugging at my mouth. "Not too long ago you were about to take my license away." I took another taste of the drink. "This place bugged?"

"No."

"Doesn't really matter. I'm glad to tell you. I intend to tumble this Penta guy. I may just take him down or I may take him out altogether. The son of a bitch tried to kill somebody I care a lot about and he laid a load of shit on me with that kill in my office and I don't let something like that go by."

"How can you find him?"

"What did you learn at Norfolk, kid?"

"Legwork, informants, psychological profiles, and on and on."

"Good for you. Only you forgot the biggest one."

"Which?"

"Experience."

"And what is experience?"

"A lot of time being aggressive, stubborn, a target and a damn fool."

"You have all that?"

"More. I'm smart."

She couldn't hide the smile. "How smart is that?"

"Enough to tell you what you want to be when you grow up."

I knew she was going to say it. "Want to bet?"

"Sure. What do you want to put up?"

She walked right into it. "Oh, you name the terms."

I took my time and put away half the drink. "If I lose," I said, "I'll tell you who Penta is."

Her eyes narrowed. "You said you didn't know . . ."

"That was then."

She was on edge now. This was something she had to know and she wasn't concerned about losing. Even if I was lying, it still didn't matter. "And if you win?"

I shrugged casually. "You take off your clothes. Here."

All of the Ice Lady's emotions were exposed in a flash, the crudity of the suggestion, the daring of the act, the shame of exposure, the desire to do the unthinkable. It was one beautiful expression.

But she couldn't lose. She said, "You're on."

I finished the drink and put the glass down. "How many guesses do I get?"

"Just one."

"Fair enough." I leaned back in the chair and looked at her. The music playing was Brahms's Hungarian Dance No. 5. "You plan to be ... no, you *intend* to be, without a shadow of doubt you know you have to be and will be ..." She wasn't breathing. She was sitting there with a strange, stark look on her face. "... the president of the United States."

The back of her hand went to her mouth very slowly. Her eyes were wide, shocked, her lovely mouth opened slightly with astonishment tinged with fear because I was completely inside her mind.

"No!" I could hardly hear her. "It's impossible. No one knows. I ... I've never mentioned it to anyone. Never. You can't possibly know this." She got to her feet slowly, putting her glass down before she dropped it. For a moment she almost lost her composure. "How did ... you know?"

"Doesn't matter."

"Yes, it does."

"Experience. I won, didn't I?"

"Yes."

"I'm waiting," I said.

"You will never mention this to anyone, never."

"Why should I?"

Her lower lip went between her teeth and she stared at me. She was wondering how she'd lost all control of the situation. Her initial plan had gotten out of hand and now she had to put her integrity on the line.

The dress was a simple but dramatic arrangement. Her hand went to her chest and found the concealed zipper. She pulled it down quickly, not for effect, but because had she not she wouldn't be able to pay her debt at all.

My Ice Lady was hurting, but determined. She took a deep breath and I knew what she was going to do next.

I said, "Don't."

Her hands held the dress she was about to pull open locked to her breasts. "It's a debt I owe," she forced out.

"Wrong. It was a dirty trick I pulled."

"Mike ... don't lie. What you said was true and no way outside of reading my mind you could have known."

"Zip up, Candace. If I really wanted you naked, I would have gotten you that way myself."

"Then why did you ... ?"

"I wanted to see if you'd stick to your word."

Her fingers reached for the zipper and drew it up, slowly this time. A tiny feeling of anger showed in the tightness of her mouth, but there was hurt in her eyes. That was something I didn't expect to see.

"You really *don't* want me, do you?"

"Don't fool yourself, honey. I thought about it the first time I saw you and have ever since. You don't have to tell me you haven't been in the sack with anybody yet . . . no woman aching for the presidency in these days had better take that chance. That much I know. But now I like what I see better than I did before." I reached for my hat and pushed out of the chair.

"Mike . . . if you had lost . . . would you have told me about Penta?"

I didn't have to lie my way out of that. I said, "The point is moot, kid. I didn't lose." I winked at her and stuck my hat on. "Thanks for the drink."

She smiled when I walked past her toward the door and just as I was reaching for the knob, she said, "Mike . . ."

I looked back and suddenly had one of those feelings that I had been here before in another time.

The Ice Lady had let her dress crumple at her feet in soft folds and she had been wearing nothing beneath it. She was nude rather than naked, not icy at all, but warm and beautiful and so alive I could see the gentle movements of her breathing. Very alive. The nipples of her breasts were proudly erect.

She smiled at me. I smiled back and opened the door.

The desk nurse at the hospital was glad to have somebody to talk to, even at midnight. Velda was still under sedation, but definitely improving.

The doctors had been in twice that day and were pleased with her progress. Yes, a police officer was still at the door and no, they never wandered off. Officers would relieve each other at regular intervals. I thanked her, hung up and dialed Petey Benson at his apartment.

As I expected, he was having a beer in front of the TV and when he recognized my voice, asked, "How'd you make out?"

"Like brother and sister," I told him.

"Yeah, I bet. What's up this time?"

"You have any connections in England?"

"Hey, England's a big place."

"Manchester, England."

"Well, there's a sportswriter on the *Manchester Guardian* I met in London at a football game. Not like our football, but like soccer ..."

"I know what you mean," I snapped impatiently. Don't steer him and Petey would go off into every odd angle. "How can I reach him?"

"Got a pencil?"

"Sure."

"Then I'll give you his number." He rustled some pages in his phone book, then read the number off to me. "I think we're five hours behind them over there. Call him a little later and you might get him in."

"Okay. I'm going to use your name."

"Be my guest. I don't suppose you want to tell me what this is all about."

"Later," I said.

Russell Graves was in and "delighted indeed" to speak to someone in the colonies. Actually, in fact, it was the first overseas call he had ever gotten, as he put it. Petey was some sort of a hero figure to him, an American crime reporter who had a fat expense account and was assigned to the really exciting cases. When I told him I was a real American private eye who was working with Petey and needed an overseas connection he got so worked up I thought he'd cream his jeans. He made sure I knew he was only a sports reporter, but I told him that crime was everywhere, even in sports, so that shouldn't stop him.

"Well, then, Mr. Hammer, what is it you wish me to do?"

"Sometime back an American was murdered outside Manchester. I don't know his name and can't describe him, but he was a federal agent working over there."

"That sounds awfully vague, Mr. Hammer."

"Possibly, but murders in your country aren't all that frequent."

"Times have changed somewhat, sir."

"I realize that. But this is an American who was killed. If it happened in the countryside somebody would be aware of it. There's one other thing . . . this kill could have been a vicious one."

"Vicious?"

"Not a clean kill. There might be something pretty nasty about it. You know what I mean?"

"Yes," he said, "I believe I do."

"Now," I went on, "there's a possibility that our government and yours are playing this matter down, but we're looking for a killer who hit over there and here, and likely will try to hit someplace else too. That's why I suggest you look outside the normal channels for anything on the murder over there."

"Is there any way I can get a story out of this? I'm sure my editor would see it in my favor . . ."

"Guaranteed, Russell. You and Petey can have it together if it works out."

That was enough for him. I gave him my home and office numbers, told him to call person-to-person and if he could expedite matters any, I'd get him tickets the next time our pro teams staged a preseason football game in a British stadium.

When I hung up, I got a cold beer out of the refrigerator, drank it down in two long draughts, as the British would say, and went to bed.

5

I parked the car a half block down from Smiley's Automotive, got out and took a look around. Lower Manhattan had a lot of areas like this, old buildings eroding away from lack of maintenance, homes to run-down shops dealing in out-of-date or surplus goods. The smell of Butyl rubber came from a tire-recapping place that had opened early. Outside their doors two guys were unloading casings from a pickup truck.

One place had a TOOL-AND-DIE sign in the window, but didn't look as if it did any business at all. There was a plate-glass shop that looked stable and another garage, just opening, that specialized in TUNE UP AND REPAIRS. A few other places looked like they were closed for good.

When I passed Smiley's I thought it was closed, but there was a light in the back and somebody was moving around. I gave the door a bang with my fist, waited, then did it again.

A voice yelled, "Take it easy, I'm coming, I'm coming." A little old guy opened the door and said, "We ain't open."

I stuck my foot in the door and put my hand against it. "You are now, buddy." I shoved it open, reached in my pocket for my wallet and gave it an empty flash and put it back.

The gesture was enough. "You doggone cops, why don't you just come down and live here?"

"No TV," I said. "Where do you live, Pop?"

"The same place I lived when the other cops were here. I already told 'em."

"You didn't tell me."

"Right around the corner. Over the grocery store. What do ya think you're gonna find? There ain't nothing here."

"It's a followup call, Pop. You know what a followup call is?"

"I know you're gonna tell me, that's what."

"It's in case you remembered something you forgot."

"Well, I didn't forget nothing."

I reached in my coat pocket for a note pad and let him see the gun in the shoulder holster. There's nothing that impresses people more than seeing a gun. "What's your name?"

"Jason." I looked at him. "McIntyre," he added.

"Address?" He gave that to me. "Who do you work for?"

"I told you guys."

"Now tell me."

"When Smiley wants things done, I work."

"What things?"

"Clean up. Sometimes run errands. Hell, I'm too old for anything else. Had to come in after the cops shoved everything around. What in hell were they looking for anyway? They said somebody beat up on a guy in here. There was some bloody spots on the floor and you know what?"

"No, what?"

"I found a tooth, a whole tooth, by damn. It was right there on the waste pile in a glob of bloody spit. Wires and all still right on it."

"You show that to the police?"

"Nah, they'd already went."

"Let's see it." He gave me a glance as if it were none of my business and I said, "Get it."

It was a tooth, all right, a single partial plate holding what seemed to be a lower canine. Part of the plastic holding the tooth had been snapped off, but the wire bracings that attached to adjacent teeth were intact.

I asked him, "What were you holding on to this for?"

The old guy threw up his hands. "Shoot, mister, them things cost money. If that guy came back looking for it, I could work a fiver out of him."

I shook my head as if I didn't believe him.

"You think I'm kidding? Last year I had a pair of glasses that got under the hydraulic rig somehow. Glass was broke, but the rims was real gold. I got six bucks for it."

"When was that?"

"I dunno. It was winter. Cold as hell out."

"Where was Smiley?"

"He took that week off. I came in before he got back to make sure the heat was up. Smiley don't like to waste no money."

"When's he coming back this time?"

"Tomorrow," Jason told me. "He don't like all this crap going on here."

"Then I'll come back tomorrow."

"What about my tooth?"

"Tell you what," I said. "If I can't find who it fits, I'll give it back to you."

"Cops don't give nothin' back."

"You're probably right," I told him.

One block over I found the neighborhood coffee shop. I expected it to be the usual dilapidated slop chute that you come across in these areas, but the little old Italian lady who ran the place had it as neat as her own kitchen. When I walked in I must have had a pleased look on my face because she laughed and said, "Surprise, eh. You are surprise. Everybody new here is surprise."

I slid onto a stool and ordered an egg sandwich and coffee.

"Bacon?"

"Why not? Sounds good."

She nodded and turned to her stove. "And the big eggs I got. No little mediums. For the men who work hard, I got extra large."

"Sounds great."

"You don't work here, no?"

"Nope. I had something to do at Smiley's, but he's not there."

"Ah, fancy man Smiley. I used to tell my Tony, Smiley was a fancy man."

She poured my coffee and I asked her, "What's a fancy man?"

She shrugged and wagged her head. "Little man, too big pants. Likes to make a big show. He wants change for a twenty for a doughnut. You want your egg over?"

"Real easy. Don't break the yolk."

She buttered the bread, laid four slices of bacon on it and deftly put the egg on top. She watched me tap the yolk with my knife, spread it over the bacon and slap the lid on it. When I took my first bite I could feel the yolk roll down my chin. She laughed. "Only the sexy men, they eat like that."

"Delicious," I told her. Then: "Guy over there said Smiley would be back tomorrow."

"Sure, he come back," she agreed. "He'll buy coffee, give me a twenty. Big shot. Him and the ponies. I told my Tony he was a no-good fancy."

"Doesn't he ever lose?"

"Smiley the fancy man? Never. He's the big shot who never loses."

I finished my sandwich, gave her the right change with a dollar tip and said, "Just so you don't figure me for a fancy man."

For another hour I walked around Smiley's block talking to the guys who worked there. Nobody seemed to care much for Smiley at all. He got some odd jobs in his shop, but nothing that would mean big bucks. It was the track that kept Smiley a step above everybody else.

One of the guys didn't even believe that. "Shit, man, he goes to the track when there ain't no track running. He likes to make like he takes a plane somewhere, but shit, he's broke before he goes. When he gets back he has a bundle."

"So he goes to OTB."

"You kidding? Smiley goin' legal to Off Track Betting? A bookie, maybe, but no OTB."

"He's got some great luck," I said.

"Balls. You know what I think? I think he's got an in with somebody. Guys what can move the odds around and tell him who to pick."

"Where would he get clout like that?" I asked him.

After he thought about it, he nodded. "Yeah. So he's still a phony. So he's got money sometimes." He spit on the ground and went back to work.

There was nothing more here to see. When tomorrow came I'd come back to talk to Smiley. Him I *wanted* to see.

* * *

Burke Reedey finished with his patients, washed up and came into the office. He sat down and rubbed his face with his hands. "Feel like a drink?"

I shook my head. "Not now."

He opened a bottom drawer, found a mini-bottle of Scotch and poured it into a glass. He toasted me with "Souvenir of the airlines," poured it down and wiped his lips. "Velda's doing fine, you know."

"They told me when I called. When will she be free to talk?"

"If you don't overdo it, you can go anytime. Her face is going to be a mess for another week, but she'll get back to normal. That blow she took was so massive we want to make sure that there is no permanent injury."

"And what would that be?"

"For one thing, a possible memory loss. So far there's no indication of that. When are you going up?"

"Tonight."

"Good. She'll be glad to see you." He grinned and added, "You know, of course, she's in love with you."

"We've been working together quite a while," I said.

"Quit working and get married. Man, you can't see the forest for the trees. That's some woman."

"In my business the longevity factor is pretty

lousy, Doctor. It makes business for you and a mess out of marriages." I changed the subject and handed him the broken partial plate from the garage.

He took it, turned it around and looked at it from all angles. "What am I supposed to say about it?"

"What are the chances of having this identified?"

"I assume you mean by the police?"

"Right."

"Well, they send dental X rays, photos of partials and full dental plates and patients' charts around the country. I don't know what percentage results in an accurate identification by the technicians who did the work, but I know there have been numerous successes." He reached out and dropped the partial in my hand. "A display this small wouldn't be easy to track. Its very simplicity is the trouble."

"Damn," I said.

"The police are pretty resourceful, Mike. Their modern technology is awesome."

"Sure, when it can be concentrated."

"Can't you narrow this down any?"

I gave him a nice grin. "Burkey-boy, you are one hell of a smart medicine man." I flipped the partial in the air, caught it and dropped it in my pocket.

Burke reached in the drawer and pulled out a small pill-sample envelope. "Let's be neat with that thing."

He watched me drop it in, seal it shut and put it away again. I told him thanks for his trouble, went down to the street and waved at a passing cab.

Pat rolled the tooth between his fingers before he laid it on top of the desk. "You come up with the damnedest things, Mike."

"Your guys didn't do a good sweep on that garage."

"Maybe if you had come right in that night the guys wouldn't have been so loose about it." I nodded. He was right on that. "What am I supposed to do with this anyway? And don't say try to trace it. We're not dealing with a dead body or a missing person, so what's the priority? There's probably been a million of these partials—"

"Hold it, Pat," I interrupted. "Just go to a pair of sources on this one. Check it out with the dental charts on FBI and CIA agents."

"Are you nuts!" Pat exploded. "You think our guys are going to pull a stunt like that?"

"Why not?"

He scanned my face. "Give me a reason. And not that bullshit about having a feeling."

"There was a finesse to the situation," I said. They were after one answer, nothing more. They didn't even try to kick the crap out of me for getting in a couple of good shots where they hurt. They left my rod alone. They had access to sodium Pentothal, they swabbed my arm with alcohol before injecting me. This is stuff guys with training will do automatically."

"Suppose it doesn't pay off?"

"You won't know until you try, will you?"

"Inquiries like this can raise a few eyebrows."

"Pat," I said, "you know and I know that all of us have strange connections in odd places. The New York Police Department is a powerhouse, baby, and when they ask, everybody listens. Just go to your connections, kid."

The hard look on his face softened into an annoyed frown and he nodded agreement. "Okay, it's a possible, so I'll put it through."

"Good."

I started to get up and he said, "Wait." He found a message slip under his desk blotter and handed it to me. "Here is a connection for you to go to, old buddy. Good luck."

Candace Amory had left a number for me to call.

"But let's keep our priorities straight first, Mike. You have something going for you, haven't you?"

"Like you said, a possible. Nothing concrete."

"Okay, let's hear it, and cut the garbage about it just being an idea."

"No problem, but tell me ... how many guys you got working on my abduction?"

"Guess."

"One."

"Right on."

"And what did he come up with?"

Pat's expression was a little shrewd. "I think we've been friends too long. You go first."

"Smiley's a middleman for somebody. That garage of his might make money, but it's a damn front."

"Can you prove it?"

This time it was my turn to grin a little. "I might be able to do it better than you can. My rules are different. Now, what do you know?"

"We're on the same track, I think. Trouble is . . . if he's on some kind of a payoff, he isn't leaving any tracks. He lives in a cheap apartment, has an old car . . ."

"And says he plays the ponies," I put in.

"Who's to say he doesn't? This time he did leave town . . . we checked him out . . . and probably did hit the track to keep his cover straight."

"You've been working, Pat."

"New York's Finest on the job," he said. "My guy tells me you've been nosing around the area down there."

Just trying to help. In this case, I'm my own client if there's any controversy about legitimacy."

"So far, no squawks. If there were it would have hit the fan by now. The Terrible Trio have been prowling around here all day going through mug shots and burning up the phones."

"What trio?"

"Coleman, Bradley and your candy lady," he said.

"I don't get State's involvement in this thing,

Pat. Why would they want a rep on the ground floor? We're dealing with a killer, not international intrigue. So Penta nailed one of their guys overseas . . . and got an ex-mobster here . . ."

"He was looking for you."

"Balls. I don't buy it. I'm no damn motive."

"Mike . . . somehow you're in this up to your ears."

"Yeah, great," I said.

"Cover your ass, pal. You prowl around like you own the city and somebody is sure as hell going to take you out."

I looked at my watch and stood up. "I won't make it easy for him."

They knew me at the hospital, but wanted to see my ID anyway. A new cop on the door scanned my PI ticket, driver's license, checking my face against the photo, before letting me into Velda's room.

"Hey, kid," I said softly.

In the dim light I saw her head turn slightly and knew she was awake. They had propped her up, the sheet lying lightly across her breasts, her arms outside it. The facial swelling had lessened, but the discoloration still put a dark shadow on her face. One eye still was closed and I knew smiling wasn't easy.

"Do I look terrible?"

I let out a small laugh and walked to the bed. "I've seen you when you looked better." I took her hand in mine and let the warmth of her seep into me. Inside, I could feel a madness clawing at my guts, scratching at my mind because somebody did this to her. They took soft beauty and a loving body and tried to smash it into a lifeless hulk because it was there in the way and killing was the simple way of moving it.

"Mike, don't," she said.

I sucked my breath in, held it, then eased it out. I was squeezing her hand too hard and relaxed my fingers. "Everything okay, kitten?"

"Yes. They're taking care of me." She tilted her head up. "I miss you."

"I know."

"What's been happening?"

I filled her in with some general information, but she stopped me. She wanted details, so I gave them to her.

Finally, after thinking a few minutes, she said, "The one you call the 'walker' . . . it was him all right."

"It's not much of an identification."

"Maybe . . . I can add something," she said. "If that caller . . . the one who made the appointment to see you . . . is the walker, or the one you call Penta . . ."

"What about him?"

"I taped that incoming call. You could get a voice-print off that and keep it for a match-up."

"Damn!" It was beautiful, all we needed was a suspect to tie into, but at least it was a plus.

Generally, incoming calls aren't monitored so the caller wouldn't be wary about leaving his voice recorded.

"How come you had it on?"

"I was getting ready to call Byers for those figures you wanted. He's always in a hurry, so I'd tape him and transcribe everything later."

"Where's the tape, honey?"

"I put it . . . in the Byers file."

"Velda doll, I could kiss you."

"Why don't you?"

I grinned at her. "Will it hurt?"

"Not that much."

I put my hands on the mattress and bent down so my face was close to hers. Her tongue slipped between her lips, wetting them, and as my mouth touched hers she closed the one eye. A kiss is strange. It's a living thing, a communication, a whole wild emotion expressed in a simple moist touch and when her tongue barely met mine, a silent explosion. We felt, we tasted, then satisfied, separated.

"You know what you do to me?" I asked her.

She smiled.

"Now I'm horny as hell and I can't go out in the hall like this. Not yet."

"You can kiss me again while you're waiting."

"No. Ill need a cold shower if I do." I stood up, still feeling her mouth on mine. "I'll be back tomorrow, kitten."

Her smile was crooked and her eye laughed.

"What are you going to do with ... that?" she asked me.

"Hold my hat over it," I told her.

The night watchman at the desk told me hello and added, "Working late tonight?"

I signed the entry list. "Just picking up some things."

"How's Velda doin'?"

"Coming along fine."

"Damn shame, that. The cops got anybody yet?"

"No, but they're working on it." I gave him back the form and headed for the elevator bank.

Only at night do you realize that an office building is almost alive. Suddenly there is no movement and what sound there is has a hollow ring to it and seems to be amplified far beyond normal. The lighting has changed and you get to thinking about funeral parlors and look for coffins in the darkened corners. What was alive during the day is dead at night.

I pulled the .45 out, threw the safety off and cocked it. I tried the door handle first, making sure it was locked, then slipped the key in and turned it soundlessly. I gave it a full ten seconds, then knelt down, shoved the door open and went in fast, hit the floor in a roll and came up against the cabinets on the far side with the gun in my fist ready to fire.

There still was no sound or movement after thirty seconds, and I felt for the light switch above my head and flipped it on. The room was empty. So was my inner office.

Had anybody been watching it would have been a good show, but I wasn't taking any chances at this point. I closed and locked the door, went to the smaller of the filing cabinets and opened the drawer with Byers' file in it. The miniature spool of tape was in the folder. At Velda's desk I flipped open the recorder and slipped the spool in, then punched the play button.

Three brief messages came on before Velda's voice said, "Michael Hammer Investigations."

The man's tone was muffled, as though he held the phone a little away from him and spoke through a handkerchief. "Yes," he said. "Would it be possible for me to see Mr. Hammer today? Noon today would be best."

"I'm sorry, but Mr. Hammer doesn't come in on Saturday."

"Is it . . . is it possible to contact him?"

"Well, that all depends. Can you tell me who is calling and the nature of your business?"

There was a brief moment of thoughtful hesitancy before he said, "My name is Lewison, Bruce Lewison . . . and my business is extremely urgent."

Velda persisted with: "Who recommended this agency, sir?"

Politely, the other voice said, "I'm afraid my business is a little too confidential to discuss. However, if you would relay to Mr. Hammer the urgency I'm sure he would understand. And I can pay for his services in advance if need be."

I could almost hear Velda's mind working. "In that case, sir, I'm sure he'd be glad to see you. I'll have him here at noon."

"I appreciate that, madam. Thank you."

The conversation ended. The voice was nobody I could recognize, nor could anybody else, most likely, but in this age of electronic technology the experts could pull a voiceprint off that tape that would make identification as exact as if he had left his fingerprints behind. I rewound the tape, took it from the case, put it in a plastic holder and dropped it in my pocket. I got a fresh reel from the drawer and put it on the machine.

When I closed the top my fingers froze to the plastic. There was no way Velda would have left the answering machine without a tape in it. A fresh one would go on before she even filed the old one.

The son of a bitch had come back. He had figured out the remote possibility of having been recorded, did a highly skilled job of opening the door locks and searching the place, the way a *real* enterprising reporter might. But he had already gotten what he came for ... the tape from the recorder.

Too bad, sucker, I thought, too bad.

He wasn't up on efficient office procedure at all. He never figured Velda would file his taped message and insert a new reel before he got there.

But then, he didn't know Velda's sensitivity level at all. Bruce Lewison my ass. She knew it was a phony name and red-flagged it for me in an off-file.

I got out of the cab at the rear of my apartment building and went down the garage ramp. I took the service elevator up to my floor, stepped out at the far end of the corridor where I had a good view of the whole area, then went to my door. The splinter I had inserted between the door and the jamb was still there, so nobody had tried to bust in.

The late news was on. I built a drink and sat in front of the TV watching everybody go through the motions of laying the city naked. Local politics was still a mess, but the mayor did his funny bit and made a joke of it. There was a street killing, a multicar accident on the East Side Highway and a tenement fire on One Hundred Twelfth Street. Almost the same as the news last night.

When I was putting some more ice in my drink the phone rang and I picked it up and said hello. A voice in an echo chamber with a British accent said, "Mr. Hammer, is that you?"

"Russell?"

"Yes, right. This is he. I have some news for you."

"Great."

"I must say, it was a bit of a go, y'know. Very difficult to get any information from the authorities except that the case was still under investigation. The people here knew that an American was killed, but didn't know why. The thing that was gruesome was the way he died. A knife in his throat was the murder weapon, but his fingers had been cut off his right hand."

"Did the press carry that?"

"Afraid not, old boy. The only one here who knew about it was the man who discovered the body. Getting him to talk wasn't easy at all. The constabulary had explicitly forbidden him to mention it to anyone."

"Then how'd you manage it?"

"Very simply, Mr. Hammer. I offered him twenty-five pounds and my vow of silence."

"Russell," I told him, "you did fine. I'll send you a check at the going rate of exchange."

"Don't forget my football tickets and the story."

"You got it, friend."

I hung up and sat back with my drink. Now Penta had an MO. He liked to chop off fingers. He took five off the agent in England and ten off the poor slob in my office. The numbers seemed to have a significance. And the chances were, Penta had left his trademark in other places as well. There was always a pattern to mutilations, always a reason for them. The big ones that hit the news generally had sexual overtones, breasts and bellies being targets for a deviate's knife, or male castration and on into animal and sometimes human sacrifices. Crazy. They were all crazy . . . but every one of them had a reason for happening.

Penta. Was there a reference to *five?* Five fingers? But there were ten cut from DiCica's hands.

It was crazy, all right, but that was what was going to trip up Penta. I finished my drink, took a shower and went to bed. I set the alarm for six and set the switch.

At seven thirty I parked two blocks away from Smiley's Automotive and walked back on the opposite side of the street. Outside the tire-recapping place a lone truck loaded with used casings was parked, the driver asleep behind the wheel. An old van rattled by and turned the corner up ahead, and that was the end of the traffic. Nobody seemed to be anxious enough about business to open early.

Smiley's Automotive was just another place on the block. It was *there.* Nothing was happening. Behind the dirty windows in the door was the dull glow of a night bulb. After ten minutes nothing had changed and I walked across the street, and only when I got up close I saw the quarter-inch gap in the personnel door where it hadn't been closed all the way.

When I nudged it with the tip of my toe it swung open, and I went in fast, the .45 in my hand, and flattened out against the wall long enough to get my bearings, then took four steps to the steel lift and crouched down behind it.

Nothing moved.

I inched my way to the other end of the lift and paused there, listening. The tiny scratching noises I heard were coming from the small office in the rear off to my left, minute hurried noises that stopped and started, then were joined by others, and when I heard the brief whistle sound I realized what I was hearing.

I got up, moved to the door quietly and the rats that were running all over the place saw me and dashed across the desk. When I flicked the light switch on with my elbow I saw all the tiny paw prints and tail streaks from the blood they had been gorging themselves on, a thickening deep red pool that oozed out of the balding head that had been smashed open with a two-foot-long Stilson wrench.

The body was still in the swivel chair, the head and arms flopped forward on the desk. Apparently that single blow had taken him out so fast he hadn't moved a muscle afterward. The eyes were still open, half a dead cigar was in the corner of his mouth, extinguished by the blood that puddled around it.

Under the right arm were two bills from a Las Vegas hotel and a used airline ticket. I could see the name on one bill and the ticket. It was Richard Smiley.

I draped a tissue around the phone, dialed 0, and when the operator came on told her I couldn't see without my glasses and gave her Pat's office number. He had just gotten in and I was about to ruin his whole day for him.

"Yeah, Mike. Now what's happened at this time of day?"

"Somebody's polished off Smiley."

"What?"

"I'm at the garage now."

"Shit. You stay right there and damn it, don't touch anything."

"Come off it, pal. All I've done was dial 0 on the phone."

"You alone?"

"Totally. Whoever did this had time to get away. The blood is congealing enough to make him dead for at least an hour. Consider that an unofficial opinion."

"You sure it's Smiley?"

"His papers indicate it." Before he could ask I said, "They were lying on the desk."

"Okay," he told me, "hang in there. We'll be right down."

I cradled the phone and looked around. I had probably five minutes before a squad car got there, and if there was anything to know I wanted it firsthand.

For a few seconds I studied the way the body was positioned, as if he had been doing something on the desk. The blow had come down at an angle, carefully placed and forcefully delivered. The killer had been in close, standing there until the right moment, then he came down with the weapon on Smiley's bald skull and demolished him with one terrible whack. The Stilson wrench was simply dropped beside the body and the killer walked out. He didn't even have to bring his own bludgeon. There were enough wrenches, crowbars and lengths of pipe in the office to handle the matter.

Whoever the killer was, Smiley had known him. Had a predawn meeting been set for a payoff? It sure looked that way. Smiley could have had the money in his hands, counting it, probably the way he had before. No reason to be apprehensive. It was a regular business deal and he was just making sure he got what was coming to him. And he got that, for sure. The killer simply retrieved the money and walked out into a lonely night that didn't even have street people to watch him go.

As professional kills go, it was a nice clean one. Just a big bang on the head and it was over. No fancy work, no revenge or bloody messages like the one in my office. Smiley still had all his fingers.

The first squad car got there in four minutes. I held up my ID for the two uniforms to see, but the driver recognized me and nodded. "You call this in?"

"Yeah. The body's in the back office. I left everything clean. All I touched was the phone under a Kleenex and the light switch with my elbow."

The officer took out his pad while the other one went inside. "Let's get the paperwork done first."

"Sure." I gave him all the personal information he needed, detailed my entry, the discovery of the body and subsequent events. As I was finishing, two more squad cars pulled in with an unmarked sedan right behind them. Pat was at the wheel, his face tight and drawn, and when Candace Amory and her boss got out, I could see why.

Pat told them to stay right there until the investigation was completed inside, spotted me and came right over. "Mike, what is this penchant you have for being around dead bodies? To hear the DA sound off you're a walking menace."

"I didn't kill anybody. Not yet, anyway."

"Given time, you will, you will. And *that's* from the mouth of our eminent district attorney. Now what happened?"

I gave it to him the same way I did to the first cop on the scene.

"And you came down here on a hunch?"

I shrugged.

"We had a surveillance unit on Smiley's house last night. He never went home."

"If he came in on the red-eye he could have come right here."

"Why?"

"Because he was one of those greedy bastards who wanted his money as fast as he could get it.

The office was as good a place as any for a payoff and the time was right."

The police photographers arrived and went inside. Pat looked at his watch and said, "You stay put."

"Where can I go?"

"Go talk to the wheels over there," he said.

"Pat . . . how come the DA isn't giving you a hassle right now? He usually likes to be right underfoot."

"I think the Iceberg Lady has a leash on him," Pat said sourly.

No introductions were necessary. The district attorney and I had met before, and if ever there was an adversarial situation, it was the one between us. He had come up out of the ranks and was in his first term of office, and to him, people like me were legislative errors in licensing who had no business in police work. He was the type who disapproved of using informers or sting techniques or anything that might open a legal case to any type of defense.

I said, "Hell of a way to start the day."

"You seem to have a knack for this sort of thing," he told me. "Care to recite the details again?"

I said no and went through the routine.

He took it all in, filing away every detail mentally. "You have a strange position here."

"You'd better believe it, counselor. I'm a principal, a finder of bodies, an authorized investigator and if the reporters get here soon, source material for a good story."

Another car drove up and parked in the middle of the street. The medical examiner got out and walked past me. With an amused smile he said, "You again, eh?"

I nodded. "Some people have all the luck."

Candace was watching the exchange closely and waited until the ME had gone inside. "I think we have things to talk about, Mr. Hammer." She didn't use my first name this time.

"I'm sure we have."

Pat called to the pair of them and waved them inside. He pushed his hat back and wiped his face with his hand. "I guess you got the picture," he said to me.

"Unless your guys turn up something else."

"Smiley wouldn't keep records of anything like this going down, but someplace there's a paper trail."

I made sure nobody could overhear me and said, "There might be something better than that."

He watched me out of the corner of his eye. "Like what?"

"If the first killer, Penta, was the one who made the appointment to make sure I was in the office, then I may have his voice on tape."

"Where is it?"

I took the cassette out of my pocket and handed it to him.

"Who else knows about it?"

"Just Velda."

He stuck the tape in his jacket pocket. "I'm going to keep this in my own department for a while."

The way he said it, I knew something was irritating him. Before I could ask him what it was, I saw Jason McIntyre sidling past on the other side of the street, his eyes wide with curiosity, but his actions reflecting the nervousness he couldn't hide. I said, "There's a guy who can identify the body, Pat."

"Where?"

I pointed Jason out and Pat called a patrolman over and told him to pick him up. The old guy almost fainted with fright when the cop took his arm, but he went along, was taken inside and came out a minute later shaking, his face a ghastly white. But he had made the ID. It was Richard Smiley, all right. Jason went to the curb and puked.

Candace and her boss came out together. He seemed to be a little glassy-eyed, but she was taking it right in stride. For a moment she looked toward me, but two trucks, remote TV units from rival networks, were coming down the street, swerved in hard and disgorged their crews with military precision. In seconds they had targeted on Candace, switched to her boss, sought out other high-priority subjects while one cameraman was trying to edge inside the building.

"How are you going to call this shot when you're on camera, Pat?"

"Usual. The investigation continues, we have a suspect, we expect an arrest shortly."

"Motive?"

"Apparent robbery will do for now. His wallet was open, empty and lying on his lap. A crumpled ten-spot was on the floor as if the killer had dropped it pulling the money out of his wallet."

"Think it'll stick?" I asked him.

"No reason why not. He'd just come back from a good day at the track, he was alone, somebody knew he'd be loaded and jumped him. Smiley might have been squirrelly to come in at that hour of the morning but that's the way he always was."

"If they buy it," I said, "the heat'll come off for a couple more days."

"But what's your explanation, Mike?"

I grinned at him and he frowned. "All I have to do is make a statement to the police. Speculation isn't my game."

Without us seeing her, Candace had come around the back and said, "But if you speculated, Mr. Hammer, what would you say?"

Pat said, "Go ahead and tell her."

I reached out and straightened the lapels of her jacket. "I'd say somebody just didn't want old Smiley in a position to identify him or his pals." I paused for a second before adding, "And that's *pure* speculation."

"Captain?" she queried.

"Miss Amory, speculation is what no cop does out loud. When the statements are made, the reports are in and I've analyzed the lot, an official announcement will be made."

She gave both of us a very speculative look, nodded, then walked away.

"Mike, old buddy," Pat said, "that broad's got a look in her eye like she wants to clean your plow."

"That's a career woman's defense mechanism," I told him. "Balls."

"She'll get them too if you don't watch out," he said.

"You want me to stick around or not?"

"Where you going?"

"Don't worry," I said. "I won't leave town."

6

Every building seems to have a forgotten corner to it that isn't good for anything at all. They are places that just sit there, empty offices with no natural light, their walls always vibrating from the elevator next to them. They smell musty and look dismal so nobody wants to occupy them. Then somebody comes along and sees that spot and to that person it becomes prime territory because it means quiet solitude where the work is intensely mental and a domain is established.

I knocked on the door, opened it and said hello to Ray Wilson. "Do you know that nobody knows where you work in this building? They kept telling me it was downstairs somewhere."

He waved for me to come in. "My own personal dungeon." He kicked a chair over to me. "Have a seat. Be right with you."

I sat down, taking in the rows of filing cabinets around me. There was an odd hum in the room, then muted voices spoke and I saw the scanner on a table in the rear. Ray was monitoring the calls to the prowl cars. Next to his desk was a new-model computer, the viewer lined with figures. There were other machines farther down, not new, but evidently competent for the work load they handled.

Ray slammed a cabinet drawer shut and walked to his desk. He perched on the corner and fired up a cigarette. "I've been wondering when you'd show up. Pat said you'd be in sooner or later."

"Now why would he do that?"

"Because I have fairly immediate access to material it would take you a month to uncover."

"Like what?" He had me interested now.

"Like the finger mutilation in your office. What does it mean?" he asked.

"It's twice as many as he took off the US agent in England."

The cigarette stopped halfway to his mouth. "How the hell did you find out about that?"

"Intelligence," I said. "Who else lost their fingers?"

He slid off the desk, walked around and sat in the old wooden swivel chair. "You're treading on dangerous ground, Mike."

"Ray . . . you got curious too. You have all the machines going for you, all the authority you need and most likely a few good connections thrown in to make things go smoothly. You could get into Interpol. Scotland Yard or the French Sûreté and as long as it's criminal activity you're after and not political, you can tap their sources. So who else lost their fingers, Ray?"

This time he took a deep drag on the butt and held the smoke down while he thought about what I said. He breathed out a thin cloud and looked at me. "I located three before it became political."

"Damn."

"A French narcotics dealer, low level, but he was skimming from the organization. The fingers were lopped off an hour before a knife stroke killed him. The second was a strange one . . . a ten-year-old kid was kidnapped from his home near Rome. The parents were immensely wealthy. The police were ineffectual and they knew they were dealing with a well-organized group of criminals. The ransom was over a million bucks in US currency. Apparently the parents took matters into their own hands, although they never admitted it. But the child was returned to them unharmed, along with a note describing where to find the kidnapper. He was tied to a chair in a barn, five fingers cut off his hand and the pointed end of a pickax slammed through his chest. The rest of the band were located and died in a police shootout."

"This guy is a wild man," I said.

"Not really." He lit another butt from the end of the old one and gulped the smoke down again. "This is no nut case. Not so far. Six months after the kidnapping a major art theft took place in Belgium. Two paintings of one of the great masters were stolen from a gallery. They were like the Mona Lisa, no way you can put an accurate cash value on their worth. At any rate, a reward was offered for their return."

"No one demanded a ransom price?"

"Apparently this theft was arranged for a private owner. It never went through. Three weeks after the robbery one painting was delivered to the gallery with a letter telling how the money was to be transferred, then the other painting would be returned. No police were involved, the gallery accepted the terms and delivered the money. The painting was subsequently returned. This time a box accompanied the picture. There were five severed fingers in it. A couple weeks later the stench of a decaying body brought the police to where the corpse was, one hand fingerless, and all the direct evidence to point to him as the thief. Whether they got his sponsor, I don't know."

"And now he's here," I said. "But this time he went for ten."

"This time he thought it was your hand he was trimming."

I shook my head. "That, Ray, is the sticker. There is no way I have any connection with this guy. That note had to be a phony. He was after DiCica to start with and I got snarled in it by accident."

"Pat gave me the hypothesis your funny friends figured out. Given DiCica's background there could be a probability . . ."

"Hell, there's logic there too, Ray."

This time Ray said no. "I don't buy it. Here this Penta character pulls a kill-crazy murder in your office. What were those other kills like?"

"Pretty well oiled," I said. "He knew what he was doing."

"But he didn't instigate the crimes, did he? Somebody sent him out looking for the perps. With the paintings it was the reward that motivated him. The killing was his signature."

"Then this guy's a hit man?"

"He's a fucking marvel, that's what. Someplace along the line my inquiries got shut down like a slammed window. I've been waiting to see if there are any repercussions upstairs, but so far this thing just sits. It's going to take a lot more weight than I got to climb a political wall."

"You sure it's gone that far?"

"Mike, I'm almost due for forced retirement. This private little police enterprise I've built into the department is going to go absolutely flat when I leave unless it captures a little glory from the money people in city government. They don't even know what they got here. The age of computers has tied this place in with every country and industry in the world like a pair of naked lovers in bed."

"Crazy, man."

"I got a feeling about this."

"So have I, Ray, so have I. But where do we pick it up from?"

He had another drag on the cigarette and coughed for half a minute. When he stopped he said, "You killed Penta, Mike. He said so himself."

"Enough, Ray. You know how long it's been since I blew somebody away. I'm sick of that stupid note."

"*You* I believe. It's this Penta who's hard to follow." He sucked on the cigarette again and coughed again. "You're still the target," he said.

"Show me a motive, then I'll believe it."

"You realize that somewhere there *is* a motive. It may be crazy and it may be out in left field somewheres, but the motive *is there*. These kills don't come from somebody who's blown his top and is walking down the street with a knife in his hand."

"So what comes next?"

"The killer is a real stalker. *Something* motivates him and he gets the job done. He's efficient, silent and completely ruthless."

"You realize what you're profiling here, don't you?"

"Sure," Ray said, "a terrorist."

"How long ago were those three murders he pulled off?"

Ray finished the cigarette and stubbed it out in an ashtray. "I wondered if you'd figure that one out. The last one was twelve years ago."

"And you think there have been more since, right?"

"A killer like that who enjoys his work doesn't stop. You know what I think?"

I nodded. "Somebody realized his potential and utilized him for their own ends."

"Smart bastard," he laughed. "When we get into the political situation the shades get drawn. Communication gets cut off. I get the feeling that sooner or later somebody is going to be asking me in for a quiet talk."

"You still going to keep at it?"

He reached for his pack and shook out another butt. "In three weeks I turn in the badge and start on my pension. No way I can leave with a situation like this wide open." He chuckled and struck a match. "Funny, in a way. I got promoted down to the bottom of the line where I like it best and I want to see the expression on some faces if this opens out to the big glory bust." He held the match to the butt and sucked on the smoke again, then rattled out a cough.

"Who else gets this research?"

"This is departmental business. Pat gets it. How he disseminates it is up to him. With you it's off the record. I guess you know that."

"No sweat. What I heard here I leave here. Thanks for the information."

"You know somethin'? For a private cop you got the damnedest connections I've ever seen. You go in and outa the department like you really belonged there. You rub asses with the hotshots, walk through the shitpiles without stepping in it and come up smelling like a guy fresh outa the barber shop."

"You jealous?"

"Nope, just curious as hell." He started to cough again and stuck the cigarette pack in his pocket.

"Those things are going to kill you," I said.

He gave me a cold-blooded grin. "Right now I'd say my chances are 'bout the same as yours."

"Sure they are," I said sourly, shaking my head.

He waved the smoke away with his hand as I headed to the door. "Stay alive, Mike," he said to my back.

There was no way I could have avoided the three reporters on the main floor. They were waiting for anyone involved in the investigation of Smiley's killing, hoping to get Pat, and I walked right into them. They would have had the official version as far as it went, but they were all old-timers and smelled a story brewing that hadn't erupted into the news yet. Two of them remembered me from a couple other wild sorties and a major court case three years ago. I had always made good copy, and now with the kill in my office and me on the scene of another one, they were trying to make a chain out of something that was only a pile of loose links so far.

I didn't lie to them. They were too good at putting things together. I didn't tell them everything either, and they knew it. What they got, the cops already had, so I didn't leave myself open.

The one reporter who had just been jotting things down when the others put the questions to me finally said, "That guy really messed up your girl, didn't he?"

My hands locked up again and I could feel the muscles in my neck go tight. "I'd like to kill that fucker," I said. My voice was suddenly harsh and I spat on the floor.

"She your girl?" he asked quietly. I caught myself just in time. He was watching me carefully, mentally recording my reaction.

"Velda works for me," I said. "We're old friends." I didn't go any further and before he could press it, Pat came in the front doors with Candace Amory and two of the reporters half-ran to intercept them. The other took his time, a wry smile tugging at his mouth. I was glad when he joined the others.

Pat and Candace dealt with them in a fast and

friendly manner, then turned them over to the PR cop who was standing by. Pat had spotted me the minute he came in and waved his thumb at the elevator. The door closed and we started up. "What're you doing here?" Pat said.

"I thought you wanted a statement."

Candace gave us both a sharp look. "Didn't you give one to the officer at the scene?" Her tone was like a reprimand.

I kept my face flat. "Not in superfine detail, lady."

"We've done this before," Pat told her brusquely. The door opened at his floor and we got off and went into his office. Pat went behind his desk, I eased into the comfortable chair by the window and Candace walked. It was an animal walk. It was a cat walk, an annoyed pissed-off strut that only a woman with a hair up her ass can do. When she stopped she stared straight at Pat and half hissed, "What's with you two?"

"Ask him." Pat didn't bother to look at her.

Her eyes reached for me next. "I don't believe this . . . this comfortable arrangement. You'd think you were ranking officer in the department . . ."

"I'm licensed."

"Where did you ever learn—"

"I've been through the FBI school, sat through all the sessions at the New York Police Academy, went through the fire marshal's school here in the city . . . want more?"

Pat was really grinning now. "Ask him how he managed it. Sure makes a good story."

"And Pat and I were in the army together," I added. "But don't think I get extra privileges."

"Horseshit," she said, and started to smile. When she walked to a chair and sat down it was still a cat walk, but now it was loose and easy.

There were two eight-by-ten glossies on Pat's desk and he handed them to me. "This thing is starting to pull in tight. Take a look."

One photo showed four barely discernible shoeprints and the other was an enlargement of one of them.

"What do you think?"

"They look like moccasins. The sole and heel are all one."

"Right, and they're different sizes ... two people."

He had me puzzled. "So?"

"See the enlargement?"

This time I looked at it carefully. There were odd geometric patterns from the sole in the print. I took a minute before it hit me. "Those are boating shoes ... nonskid soles. They come in all styles, from canvas to classics."

"That's right," Pat agreed. "Suggest anything?"

It was all going over Candace's head and the expression she wore was sheer bewilderment. I nodded. "They were pros, all right. They would be dress uppers and working lowers."

"That's not all." He picked up the phone,

punched a number and told the listener to come to the office. In two minutes the cop who did the photography came in and handed Pat two more blowups, turned and left.

He studied them for a few seconds, then let me see them. There were those soles again.

"Whoever wore those shoes killed Smiley," he said. "This one's the same size as the one on the other shot, and you know where they came from, don't you?"

I handed the photos to Candace to look at. "Those were the ones who worked me over, weren't they?" Pat was looking smug. "Damn good police work, pal."

He appreciated the compliment. "We're pretty good pros too. The manufacturer of those shoes has been identified and is sending a list of outlets that sell them, though that may not be much help. But shoes are things people keep, so we have something else to look for."

"What leads do you have, Captain?"

He didn't mention the tape I had given him. Pat could work closely with the DA, but he didn't have to get in bed with him. "There are things we are processing right now," he told her. "We should have some results shortly."

I felt like I was in the middle of a dream. Pat was talking to her and I could hear but I wasn't listening. Their voices were a far-off drone and I was sitting in the darkened garage tied to a chair, my mind stupefied from an injected drug. I was being induced to remember someone called Penta, but there was no way I could remember anything except a dream of someone behind me gagging and muttering a curse then forcefully spitting out something ugly.

Pat said, "You with us, Mike?"

I jolted alert. "Sorry about that. I was trying to remember something."

"Did you?"

"Not quite." Apparently Candace had finished her conversation with Pat during my dream sequence and she was putting on touches of lipstick. My stomach was growling, telling me I hadn't eaten all day. "Anybody for an early supper?"

"Another time," Pat told me.

I held out an offering hand to Candace. She shook her head. "Thank you, no. I'm meeting with Bennett Bradley and Mr. Coleman in a little while." Her eyes caught mine over the top of her mirror. "But I'll join you for a drink when we're finished."

"Great. I'll pick you up where?"

"At my office. Sevenish sound all right?"

"Perfect," I said. "What'll we talk about?"

She ran her tongue over her mouth to wet the lipstick. She didn't look up. "I'm sure you'll think of something."

Pat didn't have to say a word. I knew what he was thinking.

*   *   *

A hot, soapy shower turned me new again. I turned the power head from a stinging needle spray to the thudding vibrating sequence, then back to normal for a final five minutes while I shaved my beard off under the running water.

When I dried off, I pulled my Jockey shorts on, made a tall CC and ginger with a twist and turned on the phone recorder. The first call was from the dry cleaners telling me my clothes were ready. The second was from Russell Graves in Manchester, England, who wanted me to return his call. He gave me the number and I put the phone on my shoulder and dialed it.

The British phone did its double burp, rang twice, and a heavily accented voice said, "Yes, can I help you?"

"Russell? This is Mike Hammer. What's happening?"

This time he didn't sound flippant at all. "Mr. Hammer ... I think you had better know, well ... this business with the mutilated fingers?"

"Yes?"

"Twice I have been called upon by persons I suspect are from the police. They wanted to know about my interest in the ... the dead man."

"Did they identify themselves?"

I heard him swallow. "They didn't have to. They have a way about them, y'know."

"Russell, you are in England, buddy. The police don't work that way."

"These were ... a different sort of police."

"What are you talking about?"

"British intelligence agents don't work under the same rules as our bobbies."

"They threaten you?"

"Let me say . . . they were *threatening*. Only when they determined I was a bona fide reporter did they leave. The implication I got was . . . that I was an unwelcome intruder."

"Did they say that?"

"It was what they *didn't* say, y'know. I'm afraid there's something very big in the wind. They were very frightening."

"Why the call then?"

"Because . . . one mentioned, well, rather out of turn, I doubt if he was aware of it . . . not to go looking for '*the others*.' Now, he might have said '*any* others,' but I'm quite sure he said '*the* others.' In that case, there would be more."

"Beautiful, Russell, you did fine. Don't go out looking for any of them."

"Oh, you can be sure of that, Mike. I'm really not into violence. Those men were quite burly. Knew what they were about too. Thought you'd want to know, however."

I thanked him again and hung up.

I sure was in the middle of something.

They hadn't quite finished their meeting when I got to Candace Amory's office. Her door was open and I could hear their quietly argumentative voices down the hall. In a steely tone I heard

Coleman say, "In all this time there has to be *somebody* able to identify him. This one-name 'Penta' business must have some significance."

"Well, we're coordinating all the information the embassy's gathered in. We really haven't all that many men in the field—"

I interrupted him from the doorway. "Why not, Mr. Bradley?"

The interplay of glances between the three of them was quick. Candace reacted with sudden surprise and I knew she had forgotten our date for a drink. Before she could answer, Bradley said, "Why should we? A couple of killings—"

"Cut the crap, Bradley. If this Penta demands State's being on the scene we're in a big-league ball game."

"Mr. Hammer . . ." He turned sharply, facing me, a big guy carrying a lot of federal authority. He was all set to read me right out of the picture, but he wasn't that big.

I walked into the room and said, "Which couple of killings are you referring to? I can name three more civilian jobs that carry Penta's trademark and a lot of others on the political scene without any fingers." I was lying about the last bunch, but he didn't know that and I saw him stiffen visibly. He looked at Coleman quickly, then back to me. "How do you know that?"

Now it was better. He wasn't challenging me at all. He knew that someplace I had gotten information I wasn't supposed to have, and he didn't know what I was going to do with it. I wasn't somebody he could put a hold on and he had to make up his mind fast.

I gave him a simple noncommittal shrug.

Coleman cleared his throat. It had caught him off guard too. "You seem to have some unusual sources, Mr. Hammer."

I still didn't say anything.

"Did Captain Chambers tell you this?"

Truthfully, I said, "I don't think Pat even knows about it." I was full of truth these days. Ray Wilson probably hadn't had time to tell him and he didn't know Russell Graves.

"And, of course, you aren't going to tell us where you got the information from."

"What difference does it make?" I asked him. "Now we *all* know what the facts are." Candace Amory's face seemed to be frozen, but her eyes were blazing. I added, "Too bad you didn't let the lady district attorney in on your show."

Ice was in her voice too. "Yes, that is too bad. I thought we were a team."

"We were going to, Miss Amory. For the moment we thought it best to ignore the background and concentrate on the current situation." Bradley was really trying now. "Perhaps if Mr. Hammer leaves, we can put our cards on the table—"

I didn't let him finish. "Why don't you tell her you're after a terrorist, Bradley?" I ignored him then and looked at Candace. "He's a hit man, kid. A coolly professional killer who can work in the big time and enjoys signing his work with finger mutilation. Somebody took him out of his grade and put him in the political arena. Now he's over here."

Candace walked to the door, closed it, then came back to the table. To Bradley she said, "I assume this is true?"

"Generally, yes."

While the static was still in the air I said, "Why don't you put the cards on the table, people? Whether you like it or not, I'm in. There's no way you can cut me out now."

Before Bradley could stop her, Candace looked directly at him, but was speaking to me. "Mr. Bradley is the State Department's expert on this Penta person. I though his assignment was fairly recent, but it looks like he's been at it for some time now. Is that right, Mr. Bradley? Or do I reach my associates in Washington to find out?"

There was no embarrassment in Bradley's face at all. They train the State guys well. When something sours, they go with the play and take the best way out.

He talked to me too, but his eyes were on hers. "Yes, it's quite true. I have led a specially selected team to locate and seize Penta for the past eleven years. We've gotten close several times, so have the British, but every time he has eluded us. There have been nine important political assassinations credited to him, but on these there were no mutilations. Instead, there was a simple slash across the backs of all four fingers and the thumb in each case. Rather than leaving a signature, he was initialing his work. When our agent apparently surprised him in England, he reverted to his previous method of total finger amputation to show his displeasure."

"Who's his boss?" I asked him.

"It would have to be an unfriendly. Somebody funds him well."

From the side, Coleman cut in with, "We suspect that he could be somebody in a low level of politics or a police organization. The way he moves, he seems to have a great deal of insight into our activities."

"And if you must know, Mr. Hammer, it was because of the death of our agent in England that I was removed from my post and brought back to the States."

"Then why are you here?"

"Because I'm the only one who has had any previous experience with this person's operation. When Victor Starson gets here, I'll be relieved and transferred to Washington."

"Meanwhile," I reminded him, "Penta is here."

"And so are you, Mr. Hammer. Please remember that it was you he came for."

"Now we're back to square one. I'm a political zero. I have no ties to government policy in any way. I'm the one big mistake in this scenario."

"This killer hasn't made a mistake yet," Bradley said softly. "As long as his identity is an absolute mystery, all the odds are on his side."

"Buddy, he's no ghost. He's been seen by a lot of people. Trouble is, they never knew who they were looking at." I paused and looked at all three of them. To Bradley I said, "But you are wrong about him never making a mistake."

They waited to hear the rest of it, but I looked at my watch, then at Candace. "We going to get that drink, Miss Amory?"

But Coleman wouldn't let it drop. "You were saying, Mr. Hammer . . ."

"I was saying that this is a police matter in the City of New York and you'll just have to wait for Captain Chambers to release any fresh information. You ready, Miss Amory?"

Everybody left. The good-byes were fuzzy. Candace and I got in a cab and I had the driver take us to the Old English Tavern. Petey Benson was at the bar talking baseball to a yuppie type and almost dropped his teeth when he saw me with Candace.

I nudged Candace's shoulder. "Care to meet a fan?"

"Does he vote?"

"What difference does it make? You were appointed."

"One day that will change."

"He votes," I told her.

She smiled pleasantly. "Then by all means, introduce us."

Petey was a little uncertain about taking the hand she held out, but grinned and gave her fingers a squeeze. He appreciated civilian authority from an objective viewpoint, not this close. "Petey's one of the good-guy reporters, Miss Amory. Got real hidden talents."

"Wonderful," she said.

Silently, Petey was kicking my tail.

I told him, "You feel like doing me a favor, pal?"

"Nope, I don't ever . . ."

"Get into your files and get me some information on DiCica. Not his record or any late stuff. Go back as far as you can."

"Why? The guy's dead."

"Just do it, okay?"

For a second I thought he was going to tell me to forget it, but he read my eyes a second and nodded slowly. "Sure," he told me. "Only because of one thing will I do it."

"What's that?"

"We got computers and fax machines now and I don't get tied up for a week scanning old copy."

I threw five bucks on the bar and ordered beers for Petey and his baseball buddy, then went back to a table with Candace. I answered her question before she could ask it. "The killer was after DiCica or me. Now, I know all about me, and I know something about DiCica. What I want is to know *all* about DiCica."

"We *know* all about DiCica."

"Hell, kid, not even DiCica knew that. He led two completely different lives."

She waited until the waiter brought the drinks, then toyed with her glass while she put her thoughts together. She knew I was watching her, feeling her with my eyes, reading the little bits of body language that she let slip, and let her mouth go firm.

"Don't do that," I said.

Her expression questioned me.

"You got a nice, sensual mouth, kid. Don't squeeze it shut like that."

"Please!" She glanced around quickly, afraid someone had heard me.

I grinned at her. "Now talk to me, pretty lady."

This time she shook her head and smiled back. "Why do I go from hot to cold with you?"

"Because you're playing the game too, doll."

"And what does the winner get?"

"I'm not sure what the prize is yet," I told her.

She let her teeth slide over her lower lip, folded her hands under her chin and gave me a studied gaze. "You're going to be a winner, aren't you?"

I didn't answer her.

"That's what's disturbing me. Disturbing everybody. You're the piece that doesn't belong, but has to be there. As my friends say, a lousy private cop in a position they can't shove around. Why is that, Mike?"

A slight shrug was the best I could do.

"My boss defers to Captain Chambers. He recognizes his professionalism and appreciates his opinion. Somewhere you have a niche in all this and nobody but you seems to know where it is." She paused dramatically. "Where is it?"

"Right in the middle of the shitpile," I said.

"Gross."

"Not really. You ever been shot at?"

Her head made a slight negative movement.

"When it happens," I told her seriously, "you'll know what I mean."

"But you'll still be a winner."

"Candace honey, whoever stays alive the longest wins. Right now something is happening and nobody wants to spell it out. We have federal agencies sniffing around, the State Department playing footsies in a murder case because they're afraid they might screw up the political scene. Right now all that's a lot of crap. We're working on a murder, a killing that comes under the jurisdiction of the New York Police Department."

"No murder is simple."

"And a kill isn't complicated," I reminded her. "Only the motives are complicated."

She took her hands down now, settling back in her chair. Her head tilted slightly and she gave me that odd stare again. "See . . . that's the other thing about you that's puzzling."

This time I waited.

"Someone wanted to kill *you*. Most likely he still wants to kill you and you don't seem to be scared a bit."

"Don't fool yourself."

"You're scared?"

"Not the way you'd count scared. I'm cautious. And you have to be alive to be scared."

"That's a thought."

"I'll give you another," I said. "Be scared, but don't let your hand shake."

"Later I'll ask you to explain that." She snapped her pocketbook open and pulled out a vanity, glanced at the mirror and put it back.

"Later?"

"After you take me home," she said impishly.

They forget sometimes, these beautiful women. There are times when they can lift their skirts up to their eyebrows and nobody will even blink because they did it in the dark, and right then my eyes were closed.

When the cab pulled up to her building and the doorman did his little sprint, I said, "When your hand shakes, you miss the target, kitten."

She glanced at me, frowning, and asked, "Is your hand shaking?"

"It doesn't matter, honey. I'm not aiming."

I kissed the tip of my finger and stuck it on the end of her nose.

This time she smiled and got out of the cab. It wasn't an impish smile at all.

7

The workout at Bing's Gym let me tear at something physical for a change. Weight machines were enemies I could push and shove at, my jaws clamped hard in the effort. I could pound at the heavy bag and rap the hell out of the light one, and even if it wasn't the real thing, there was something therapeutic about it that made me feel better.

I would have kept it up, but Bing reminded me that I was overdoing it for this session and ushered me into the steam room with a towel wrapped around my middle. Nobody else was there, so I sat and let my mind drift through the details of an old hardcase being mutilated and killed in my office.

One lousy murder and the whole world fell apart. The DA's office is in, the FBI is in, the CIA is in, the State Department is in, because a guy they call Penta took out a wacko hood. And that put me in too.

But there was one thing that only I knew for absolute certainty ... I really wasn't in at all. There was no way at all that I could have any involvement with the killer. Even if he was the Penta everybody was after, *he* was after nobody else except DiCica. It sure as hell wasn't me.

Question. *Which* DiCica? The old hit man he was before he had memory smashed out of his skull? In that case, the motive was pure revenge. But why wait so long? DiCica hadn't been in hiding. Even the mob boys knew where he was. Right now Pat would have his inquiries in the works and Petey would be working from another end. Something could show up here ... possibly.

DiCica with his memory back could be something else. The mob didn't care about him as a person. All they wanted was what he had that could bring pressure on their organization. They *could* kill him, but that left his information liable to a possible discovery. Their misconception that he had contacted me for assistance meant that they didn't order the kill.

So ... another part of the organization, an upstart group or person wanting to get control or possibly another family entirely, knew DiCica had flashes of memory recall and went after him.

In that case, did the torture session get it out of him?

Who set up the appointment to meet me in my office? Could that have been legitimate and the guy scared off by the action that day? Logical and possible.

The screwy thing was the trademark mutilation by somebody named Penta our government and the British government seemed to know all about, and it sure wasn't likely that someone in the mob circles was able to contact anybody working on Penta's level.

I let it run through my mind again and the only answer I could come up with was that somebody had picked up some stray facts about Penta and did a duplicate, but more elaborate job of mutilation on the DiCica kill to throw in the most beautiful red herring I ever saw.

And I still was in the middle of it.

After a shower I got dressed and grabbed a cab to the hospital. This time the overnight parkers had left cleared space and there was no Mercedes parked with wheels turned away from the curb. Oddly, I wondered what my muggers' options would have been if I had grabbed a cab at the entrance that night.

Downstairs I picked up a vase of flowers, took the elevator up to Velda's floor and walked to the desk. For one second I almost dropped the flowers. Pat was there talking to Burke Reedey and all I could think of was something had happened to Velda. When he half turned, saw me and nod-ded agreeably, I knew there was no trouble.

"What're you doing here?" I asked him.

"Same as you, pal, bringing flowers to a friend." But he knew what I had been thinking and added, "She's okay."

I glanced at Burke for confirmation and he grinned. "It's a good recovery, Mike. We had her for some other tests this morning and the prog-nosis looks fine."

"Can I see her?"

"Sure, but she's asleep. Leave your flowers and we'll tell her you were here."

Even though the cop on the door saw me talk-ing to Pat, he waited for him to nod okay before he let me in. I put the flowers down quietly, then stood beside the bed watching her. The swelling had gone down some and the discolor-ation had taken on a different hue, but the im-provement was noticeable. Her breathing was strong and regular, and I said, "Sleep well, kit-ten," in a barely audible whisper.

Pat and I found the visitor's lounge, got some coffee and a table away from the main crowd. "You look like something's bugging you," I said.

"I spoke to Ray Wilson this morning."

"And now I'm in deep shit, I suppose."

"No more than usual."

"What's the beef then?"

"Just cool the use of departmental facilities,

Mike. The word has come in loud and clear. This Penta business is being taken out of our hands."

"The hell it is," I told him. "The DiCica murder comes under NYPD jurisdiction."

"Not when Uncle Sammy thinks otherwise."

"So why tell me about it?"

"Because you're still the fly in the ointment. You're a principal in the case and even though you're licensed under the state laws, you're still a civilian, a US citizen, and there's nobody harder to keep quiet than one of our own."

"You can do better than that, Pat."

"Okay, our CIA pal, Lewis Ferguson, has asked for an audience in"—he looked at his watch—"forty-five minutes."

"Where?"

"In one of those cute little places the State Department reserves for quiet conferences. Take your time. Finish your coffee."

Pat had an unmarked car and we drove up Sixth Avenue to the Fifties, parked in a public garage and went into the side entrance of the half-block-wide building. The elevator took us up to the ninth floor and we turned left to the frosted glass doors marked SUTTERLIN ASSOCIATES, ARCHITECTS.

Inside, a glass booth surrounded the receptionist, and when Pat spoke to her through the cutout in the window, she told us to wait, spoke into the phone, and a minute later a young guy in a business suit with the body language of the State

Department came out, ushered us down the hallway and knocked on an unlabeled door, waited for the buzzer to click it open and waved us in.

Bennett Bradley and Ferguson were there already, Bradley behind his desk and Ferguson pacing beside him, ignoring three chairs already positioned. There was no handshaking, just perfunctory nods, and we all sat down at once.

Bradley didn't waste any time. He leaned forward on his desk, his fingers clasped together, the expression on his face as if his shorts were too tight. "Gentlemen," he started, "before we begin, I want it understood that this meeting, and what is said here, is strictly confidential. Three of us represent government agencies and understand that position, so to you, Mr. Hammer, I want to make myself clear. Is that understood?"

I said, "I hear you."

"Good. I believe Mr. Ferguson has something to say."

The CIA agent shifted in his chair to face Pat. He reached in his pocket and took out an envelope I recognized right away. "Captain Chambers, I have an item here that was routed through our office for identification."

He dumped the tooth I had found into the palm of his hand.

Pat's face hardened and he said tightly, "I was supposed to get a report in my office."

"Let's simplify things," Ferguson said. This

time he looked at me. "I understand you found this."

I hedged a little. "I came by it, yes."

"How?"

"Let's say I'm in the business of looking for clues. I was a victim of a crime of aggravated nature and made it my business to look for my assailants. That is what is called a clue."

"I don't need sarcasm, Mr. Hammer."

"None intended," I said soberly. The hardness eased out of Pat's face.

"You assumed this came from the mouth of an assailant?"

"Something did. This was the only thing that could have."

"And you took it right to Captain Chambers."

"Correct." I knew what was coming and got there first. "The mugging on me wasn't any street crime, so don't let's beat that dead horse. This went down as a very knowledgeable venture by people who knew all the ropes. They had teamwork, knew drug handling, didn't bother to confiscate my money or weapon ... hell, they even wore spook shoes that could handle any surface efficiently and quietly."

"You are referring, of course, to the CIA?"

Pat spoke up and said, "That's where the identification finally came from then, didn't it?"

Ferguson took off his glasses and rubbed his eyes. "Yes." When he had gathered his thoughts, he went on: "The recipient of that partial had the work done at a government facility after he lost it on a CIA operation. It was listed in his file and recorded on the computers."

"Who was he?" Pat asked.

When Ferguson didn't answer immediately, I said, "Want me to leave the room?"

A touch of scorn was in Ferguson's voice. "I don't think that would make any difference at this point, would it, Captain Chambers?"

"You said it in the beginning, pal. He's in this pretty damn deep and if he wants to make anything public he can do it. Just remember that he's still a good guy."

"Well put. All right, the partial belonged to an agent named Harry Bern. He was an old hand who came into the agency in 1961. He had a military background, was well rated but considered a little reckless out on assignments. When there was all that fury about extremes in our covert operations, certain agents considered touchy were released. He was one of them."

Pat said, "I suppose you checked his passport?"

Ferguson seemed surprised at that. To him cops weren't expected to think that far ahead. "He made numerous trips abroad. Apparently he's in this country now."

"Apparently," I muttered. "And he's not alone."

This time Ferguson squirmed in his chair again. "Another one we released *was* his partner, Gary Fells. They came in together and they went out together. They had almost identical background and personality profiles."

For the first time Bradley let out a *hrumph* to get our attention and when he had it, said, "Their quizzing you, Mr. Hammer, as to the whereabouts of Penta is what brings the State Department's interest into the picture."

"You can't locate either of these guys?" I asked.

"Remaining invisible if they have to is one of their specialties."

"Good training."

"Should be. They were in the first cadre General Rudy Skubal commanded."

Neither Pat nor I showed any change of expression, but we both knew what the other was thinking. General Skubal wasn't new to me at all. A long time ago he had tried to recruit me into his organization, even going to the trouble of having Pat put some pressure on me. Old Skubie, I was thinking, who took himself and the other tigers, as he called them, deep behind enemy lines for twenty-two months, a wild bunch of trained fighters fluent in Slavic languages, who raised complete hell with enemy communications until they rejoined with American units after the Normandy landing.

Most of those tigers went into frontline field work with the CIA in its early days and became shadow legends with government spooks.

"Where do we go from here?" Pat asked.

Bradley unclasped his fingers and made a steeple of them. "Nowhere. That is, *you* don't. As of now, the police department is being removed from the case. Of course, Captain Chambers, you know what that entails, don't you?"

Pat nodded, saying nothing.

"As for you, Mr. Hammer, your total silence is required. Not requested, but demanded. There will be no more investigating the Penta affair or your assailants since this all will be in the hands of federal agencies. The nature of this case is so sensitive that the fewer involved the easier it will be to process. Now, are there any further questions?"

I said, "Is looking into the murder of Anthony DiCica any part of the Penta business?"

Bradley unsteepled his fingers and gave a shrug. "I can't see what DiCica has to do with it, Mr. Hammer. Penta was after *you*."

"Thanks a bunch," I said. "Since I'm to be the quiet target then, do I get any cover?"

"I may sound callous, Mr. Hammer," Bradley told me, "but you've already made your sentiments very clear. You prefer to remain unguarded. Now, just to make sure we all understand your position, do you or do you not prefer a guard? I ask this because in your way, you too are a professional and licensed to carry firearms."

"Just let me take my chances, Mr. Bradley. I get nervous when people are watching me."

"So be it," he said and stood up. The meeting was over.

When Pat and I got to the street, he said, "You got to go anywhere?"

"No, but I'll walk you to the garage."

"Sure, then maybe you can tell me about that bit with DiCica."

"Come on, Pat, we're both thinking the same thing. It *could* have been DiCica he was really after and anything else was a sham. What have you got on the guy?"

We had stopped on the corner and Pat checked his watch. "I'm going off duty. How about a beer?"

"How can you go off duty? It's afternoon."

"I'm the boss, that's how."

"Fine, a beer sounds great and Ernie's Little Place is right here. You ever been in Ernie's?"

"No."

"Good. Neither have I."

Over the beer Pat told me about Anthony DiCica. He had a listing of all his arrests, convictions that were a laugh, and the victims he was suspected of killing. Every dead guy was involved in the mob scene and two of them were really big time. Those two were hit simultaneously while they ate in a small Italian restaurant. It was suspected by the police that it was more than a social dinner. It was a business affair and the killer, after shooting both parties in the head twice, made off with an envelope that had been seen on the table by a waiter. Following the hit there had been an ominous quiet in the city for a week, then several more persons in the organization either died or were mysteriously missing before a truce seemed to be declared. It was two weeks later that Anthony DiCica's head collided with pipe in a street brawl.

"Let's make a script out of this, Pat."

"Okay," he agreed. "Our boy Anthony went a little bit further when he hit those mob guys. He knew they were plotting against his employer and grabbed the papers. When he saw what he had, he knew he was in a position of power, but didn't quite know how to handle it, so hid it somewhere." He paused. "Now your turn."

"The mobs turned on themselves thinking of a double cross somewhere, then realized what had happened and cooled it. It took a couple of weeks to locate our Anthony, but they went a little overboard in bringing him in and cracked his skull. After that he was no good to anybody. They still needed his goods and had to wait for him to come out of the memory loss before they could move . . ."

Pat lifted his beer and made a silent toast. "We really took his place apart, you know."

"No, I didn't know. What did you find?"

"Zilch. There were no hiding places at all. We even tried the cellar area. If he had anything at all, it's someplace else."

"Now what?"

"We wait the way we usually do," he told me.

I grinned at him. "Balls. When are you going to ask me?"

He grinned back and said, "Okay, wise guy, when are you going to see General Skubal?"

"Soon. Since you're off this case I go alone, but there's no reason why we can't have a few talks together later, is there?"

"None at all."

"And I'm not investigating the Penta affair at all. Just seeing an old friend. Right?"

"Right."

"And the next time old Bradley boy *demands* I do something, I think I'll rap him in the kisser with a civilian citizen hook."

"Good thinking. You know where Skubal is?"

"I have his address in my office. I'll get it tonight."

We finished our beers and when Pat left I made two calls looking for Petey before I found him in his office at the paper. He told me to come on over. He sounded excited.

Until I saw his office, I hadn't realized Petey Benson's status at the newspaper. Most of the working reporters had a desk with a console in the quiet bedlam of the main section, but Petey had his own room, not a compartment, with a door that closed and his own bank of filing cabinets.

"Man," I said. "I thought you did all your work out of barrooms."

"That's all eyewash for the peasantry."

"You've ruined your image, pal."

"Nope. Been around too damn long to do that. What you see here is seniority at work. Plus sheer expertise, of course. Technology and computer chips rule the system these days and he who has the most gadgets wins. Wait till you see what I've come up with."

I tossed my hat on an old Smith-Corona typewriter and pulled a chair up next to Petey. "You have a work-up already?"

He nodded. "We're lucky we're dealing in areas that have good terminal systems. You know anything about computers?"

"Very little."

"Okay, let me brief you a little. In backtracking DiCica, I was able to get into records of public information, had some friends on the other end do a little legwork and between the FOI Act and the power of the press, we've got some history on Mr. Anthony DiCica. Ready?"

"Hit it."

Petey's fingers moved over the keyboard and the console came alive. "Where do you want to start?"

"All right, we'll go for basics." Then he brought Anthony Ugo DiCica up in green electronic reality. Born January 2, 1940, of Maria Louisa and Victorio DiCica in Brooklyn, New York. Victorio was a cabinet maker by trade, a World War II veteran honorably discharged in 1945. Maria

DiCica had two stillbirths There were no other children. Anthony graduated Erasmus Hall High School, June 1958, worked one year in Victorio's cabinet shop, then left and was arrested for the first time a year and one week later.

"How do you like it, so far?" Petey asked me.

"He made the streets pretty early. Pat's got his rap sheet, so skip that part and stay with the personal stuff."

Petey hit the keys again. "His father was killed in a holdup shortly afterward, as you see. Now, here's an excerpt from the *News* about the murder of a man suspected of having killed Victorio. He was even wearing Victorio's watch. Anthony was picked up and questioned, but released for lack of evidence. However, the word was that Anthony found the guy and hit him."

"He discovered his profession, didn't he?"

"More than that," Pete said, "he found a patron. Juan Torres."

I knew the name, and it hit me with force. "Now we're into the heavy cocaine scene."

"You'd better believe it," he agreed. "You know where Torres stood with the organization?"

"He was a damned lightweight for a long time, I remember that. Something happened that pushed him right up the ladder."

Pete nodded, chewing on his lower lip. "He'd just disappear for months at a time and when he showed up he was a little bit bigger. We finally figured out. Juan Torres was a *finder*. You know what that is?"

I shook my head.

"He's got family scattered all through Mexico and South America. A million cousins, you know? He's got that touch, and where there's a coke source he taps into it. He was a nobody, a nothing, but maybe that's how he made it work. The way prices are on the street, no operation was too small to tap into. Torres got the leads, made the deals and the organization moved him up. Oh, he was a damned good finder, all right. He was right inside the Medellín cartel when it first started."

Reaching across me, Petey picked four printed photos off his desk and handed them to me. In each one Juan Torres and Anthony DiCica were in close conversation against different backgrounds, obviously very familiar with each other. Here DiCica was dressed in expensive outfits, jewelry showing on both hands.

Again Petey keyed the board and brought up bills of sale and records of deeds to two houses. "DiCica was the sole support of his mother. She still lives in the Flatbush house enjoying an income from two dry-cleaning establishments he bought for her years ago."

"What about the other one?"

"A two-family place. Both rentals of long standing. The house was in his name, the rentals went to his mother. In the terms of his will she inherits the houses."

"Does Maria know what happened to her son?"

"Here's a copy of a report on her. When Anthony was in that trauma following the beating, she assumed he would die. She collected his belongings and only saw him once after that when he was released. He didn't even know her. All he remembered was something his papa had made, she said." He erased the screen and brought up another report, a letter from the medical supervisor in the hospital that attended to Anthony. He concluded that DiCica had absolutely no memory of his previous life, his mental faculties were severely impaired in certain areas, but he was capable of leading a satisfactory, if minimal, existence.

"What are you saving for me?" I asked him.

"Somebody else was keeping a watch on both those houses," he told me. "Look at this." Two minor items from the *Brooklyn Eagle* appeared. The home of Mrs. Maria DiCica had been burglarized, but nothing seemed to have been taken. The elderly lady and her live-in housekeeper had been locked in the pantry while the ransacking went on. The dateline was two days after Anthony had been admitted to the hospital.

One day later a minor squib reported an attempted robbery of another house, where the residents downstairs were trussed up and gagged while the robbers prowled through the premises before doing the same thing to the upstairs apartment where the residents were away.

"Both those houses belonged to DiCica," Petey said. "However, since nothing was reported stolen, they were after something else entirely. Now," he said with emphasis, "check this one out."

The headline was bigger this time, under a partially blurred photograph of a pair of frightened old ladies. For the second time in a month their home had been entered and this time the women had been bound, their mouths taped shut, and kept unceremoniously on the kitchen floor while the intruders went about systematically tearing their house apart. Apparently they found nothing. Neighbors reported that street speculation assumed the DiCica woman to have a horde of cash in the house since the ladies lived so frugally.

Before I could say anything, Petey keyed the console and grinned. "Don't ask me how I got this." It was a copy of a bank statement. The amount was over three hundred thousand dollars, all in the name of Maria DiCica. Deposits were regular and automatic from several sources. "Our boy Anthony had set his old mother up in fine fashion. So, what were the houses being burglarized *for* and who did it?" He sat back and looked at me. "Or should I ask?"

"I can give you an off-the-record opinion, Petey, but that will have to do for now."

"Good enough."

"DiCica had some devastating information on the mob. He hid it somewhere before he was clobbered."

With a look of finality, Petey shut the console down. "End of case. It died with Anthony."

"The hell it did," I said. "Somebody in the organization thinks DiCica suddenly remembered and dropped his secret on me."

"Brother!"

"So if it dies, it'll die with me."

"Only you're not dead yet?"

"Not by a long damn sight."

"But they got pressure on you, I take it?"

I nodded. "The bastards as much as said it was my ass if I don't produce."

"Shake you up?"

"I've been in the business too long, kiddo. I just get more cautious and keep my .45 on half cock."

He watched me frowning, grouping his thoughts. "That mutilation of DiCica could have been a message to you then."

"It's beginning to look like it," I said.

"What do you do now?"

"See how far I can go before I touch a tripwire."

"You don't give a damn, do you?" he said.

"About what?"

"Anything at all. You don't want any backup, no protection . . . you want to be out there all alone like a first-class idiotic target."

I shrugged.

"There's a lot more of them than there are of you, kiddo." I watched him and waited. He finally said, "They know how you are, Mike. You're leaving yourself wide open."

I felt that tight grin stretch my lips and said, "That's the tripwire *I* set out."

When she answered the phone, I said, "Would you really like to be president?"

There were three seconds of quiet and I knew she was studying the way I had said every word.

"There are a lot of obstacles on that road."

"I think I can clear a few of them out."

"How?"

I looked at my watch. "I'll be at your place in fifteen minutes."

All I had to do was walk around the corner and I made it in five. The doorman nodded, called Candace's apartment, then told me to go up. As I expected, I caught her in the middle of getting ready, obviously flustered at being half-dressed.

"You're a real bastard," she said. "Come on in."

I tossed my hat on a chair and followed her into the living room. She walked against the light and for a brief moment her naked body was silhouetted through the fabric of her housecoat and she did a half turn, looking back at me impishly, and I knew she was well aware of what she was doing.

"Like?" she asked.

"Cute."

"Just cute?"

"Kiddo, you are one helluva broad, as they used to say."

"Oh?"

"Especially in the buff."

"But you've only seen me once in the buff."

"It made an impression then too." I grinned at her. "Now go finish dressing."

"That I will do, believe me." She held out her hand and took mine. "You, Mike, are going to sit and watch and tell me all about the presidency." Without any hesitation, she led me toward the bedroom, ushered me in and pointed to a satin-covered chair next to her vanity. "And, of course, you are going to be a gentleman. You realize that, don't you?"

"Certainly." She was playing my game right back at me and my voice sounded hoarse. I sat down, but I wasn't comfortable.

Women are born clever. They begin life as little girls who have an instinct base that turns little boys inside out. They never seem to lose any of it, just getting better every day. They can comb their hair or put on lipstick in a way to make any guy feel a sultry ache in his groin, and now I had to watch her sitting there, deliberately opening the housecoat around her shoulders, letting it slide down to her elbows so that it lay across the fullness of her breasts, seeming to balance on her nipples. She studied herself in the mirror, her tongue licking out to wet those luscious lips before she touched them with a feathery brush end.

Her reflected glance met mine. "You were saying?"

"The police have been pulled off the Penta case."

"Our office was notified." She did the trick with her tongue again.

"If you ... and I mean you personally ... suddenly came up with something very explosive that would put you in the headlines even bigger than you expected when you busted into this affair ..."

Her eyes held mine again.

"It's another step up. The DA's office is next."

She took the hairbrush now, running it through the blond silkiness. It made a quiet, snaky sound and the muscles played very gently under her skin with the movement of her arm. The back of the housecoat slid down almost to her waist.

"Your office isn't the police department. It's still an investigative agency if it chooses to be."

Her eyebrows arched an affirmative and she put the hairbrush down on the vanity, studied herself again and stretched herself, arms out, fingers splayed in an odd theatrical gesture. She crossed one leg over the other, the gown falling away carelessly, leaving one side nude to the hip.

I said, "You have the intellect and the machinery to do something I need and do it fast. The cops have snitches out there you can reach if you play your cards right. Most likely you already have programs in place you can tap for the information I want."

She seemed to glide around on her seat until she faced me, the movement an instinctive feminine device that shocked a man's nerve endings, making me feel as if I were giving up to a slow drowning. Then a survival instinct jerked me back and I watched while she folded her hands in her lap, the motion letting the housecoat fall all the way, so she sat there, seemingly unconscious of the fact that the lovely swells of her naked breasts were mine to see.

She smiled and I said, "You're a pretty beastie, lady."

"Are you disturbed?"

"Not that much."

"You lie, Mike."

"Nicely, I hope."

"Yes. Very nicely. Now, what is it you want of me?"

"Something has our local organized crime group bent out of shape. It's big enough to squash them if it gets out and big enough to kill for to keep it quiet."

She said, "You'd better explain."

"It started with Anthony DiCica," I told her,

then laid the details out for her one by one. She let me finish without saying a word and when I got to the end she unconsciously pulled the robe up around her again, frowning in thought.

She tilted her head at me, her eyes carefully shrouded. "No games?"

"Straight, kid."

"I'm simply an assistant district attorney."

"Nevertheless, you have the clout. Your boss has enough on his desk to keep him busy. All he wants is to get into court anyway. The legwork isn't his speed."

Candace nodded and asked, "Will Captain Chambers cooperate?"

"Why not? Interagency cooperation isn't active participation. He'd like to screw that State Department patsy anyway."

"Oh, Bennett Bradley is all right. He's pretty disappointed at not having found Penta after all these years. When all of a sudden the name showed up here ... well, you can imagine how he feels, especially with a replacement for him due."

"Well, hell, he doesn't give a damn what we do about DiCica anyway. All he wants is one last clear shot at this Penta character. When can you get things started?"

She got to her feet before I could and smiled down at me. "The first thing in the morning, Mike."

Her tongue made her lips wet and she held out her hands and when I took them, she pulled gently and I stood up, feeling her fingers kneading my shoulders.

"Where do people like you come from, Mike?"

"Why?"

Girls can do strange things with their clothes too. With barely a movement, everything can suddenly fall away and they are naked and bare and nude all at once, the poutiness of their flesh pressing against your clothes like a hot iron, and they can squeeze themselves into the forbidden areas of your body the way water follows the contours of the earth.

Her mouth was soft, warm lips so cushiony and alive, feeling and tasting that it was like a kiss within a kiss. I enjoyed the flavor of her, the pillowed sensation of being enfolded by nakedness, and when it got too much, I pushed her away gently.

I knew what the look in her eyes meant. I knew what her smile meant. I grinned at her and took my lumps because she was getting back at me for the last time.

"You're the real bastard," I said.

The corner of her mouth twitched. "Uh-huh."

I took a long look at her standing there, soft, sensual musculature that was never motionless, the light outlining the gentle ripples of her body.

"Think we can start over?" I asked her.

She smiled. There was a glint in her eyes. "Why not?" she said.

I got my hat from the chair and got out of there. Downstairs there was a chill in the air and New York was getting that funny smell back again.

8

I had the cabbie drop me at the corner and picked up a late evening paper from the kiosk. There was a mist in the air and the streetlights had a soft glow around them, and lighted windows in the apartments were gently blurred. It was the kind of night that dampened street sounds and put a dull slick on the pavement.

The doorman at my place generally paced under the marquee, but tonight I couldn't blame him for staying inside. I hugged the side of the building out of the wind, moved around the garbage pails outside the areaway that ran to the rear and saw the feet inside the glass doors as the guy jumped me from behind.

Damn. The second time.

One arm had me around the throat and a fist was ready to slam into my kidneys, but I was twisting and dropping at the same time, so fast the fucker lost his rhythm and went down with me. His arm came loose and he rolled free, and I forgot all about him because the other one had come out of the hallway with a sap in his hand ready to lay my skull open. I let the swing go past my face and threw a right smack into his nose, saw his head snap back, then put another one into his gut.

This time everything was working right. The guy behind me came off the sidewalk thinking he had me nailed. I didn't want any broken knuckles. I just drove my fist into his neck under his chin and didn't wait to see what would happen. The boy with the sap was still standing there, nose-stunned, blood all over his face, but not out of it at all.

You don't have to waste skin on guys like that at all. I kicked him in the balls and the pain-instinct reaction was so fast he nearly locked onto my foot. His mouth made silent screaming motions and he went down on his knees, his supper foaming out of his mouth.

The doorman was just coming out of it, a lump already growing on the side of his head. "Can you hear me, Jeff?"

He grimaced, his eyes opened and he nodded. "That bastard . . ."

"I have them outside. You give the cops a call."

"Yeah. Damn right."

The big guy I had rapped in the throat was trying to get away. He was on all fours scratching toward the car at the curb. I took out the .45, let him hear me jack a shell into the chamber and he stopped cold. That old army automatic can have a deadly sound to it. I walked over to him, knelt down and poked the muzzle against his head.

"Who sent you?"

He shook his head.

I thumbed the hammer back. That sound, the double click, was even deadlier.

"We ... was to ... rough you up." His voice was hardly understandable.

"Who sent you?"

His head dropped, spit ran out of his mouth and he shook his head again.

Hell, neither one of them would know anything. Somebody had hired a pair of goons to lay on me, but they would sure have something to say to me about it.

"Why?" I asked him. I kept the tone nasty. I rubbed the gun harder against his temple.

All the big slob had in his eyes was fear. "You sent ... the guys ... a bullet."

I heard the siren of a squad car coming up Third Avenue. "How much did they pay you?"

"Five hundred ... each."

"Asshole," I said. I eased the hammer back on half-cock and took the rod away from his head. A

grand for a mugging meant the victim would be
wary and dangerous and these two slobs never
gave it a thought. I gave him a kick in the side
and told him to get over beside his buddy. I
didn't have to tell him twice.

Wheels squealing, a car turned at the corner
and the floodlight hit me while it was still moving. The cameraman came out, rolling videotape,
a girl in a flapping trenchcoat right behind him,
giving a rapid, detailed description of what was
going on into a hand mike, and I even let New
York City's own favorite on-the-spot TV team
catch me giving the guy another boot just for the
hell of it.

When the squad car got there I identified myself, gave my statement and let the doorman fill
in the rest. The two guys had waited near the
curb nearly an hour, spotted me at the corner,
then one came in, grabbed the doorman, waited
until the other jumped me and laid a sap on the
doorman's head before joining the fun. Luckily,
the sweatband of his uniform cap softened the
blow. Both the clowns had knives in their pockets along with the old standby brass knuckles
and a blackjack. It took one radio call to get an
ID on them and they were shoved, handcuffed,
into the rear of the car.

Enough of a crowd had collected to make it an
interesting spot in the late news coming up and
the girl said, "Any further comment on this, Mr.
Hammer?"

At least she remembered my name.

"They just tried to mug the wrong guy," I said. Then I winked into the lens and walked away.

Upstairs I called Pat, but somebody had already given him a buzz. I ran through the story again, then added, "It's all coming back to DiCica, buddy. They're making sure I know they're watching."

"You don't scare them, Mike."

"If they think I have access to what Anthony had I can sure shake them up. Did Candace Amory get in touch with you?"

"Sly dog."

"That's what Peppermint Patty says to Charlie Brown."

"What?"

"Nothing."

"Shit, you're going nuts, y'know?"

"How about Candace?"

"She'll stay busy. I assigned two damn good men to clue her in."

"Good."

"Listen, buddy . . . you have a problem."

"No way. I'm going to hit the sack."

"You see the time? That TV newscast will be on in one hour. That's how fast they can get that tape in . . ."

"So?"

"If Velda sees it, she is going to be upset as hell."

"Baloney, I did a funny at the end."

"They edit, idiot. They'll keep it hard and tight as they can. You know those two."

He was right. I said, "Look, I'll grab a cab and head up there."

"I'm closer," he told me. "I'll see if I can get there first."

"Keep her quiet."

"Will do."

I hung up. This time I took my own trenchcoat when I went back out into the night. It was a heavier mist now. Soon it would start to rain.

It was faster getting to Velda's room from emergency admitting, so I had the cab drop me off there. I went through the handful of people waiting to be helped, pushed through the double doors, took the stairs two at a time to the floor I wanted and half ran down the corridor.

The cop on duty was the one who had checked me out before. He grinned and waved to slow me down, his motions indicating everything was okay. I came to a walk to get my breath back and stood there a second, listening. I looked at my watch. The show would be running, but there was no sound from the room at all.

"What's all the hurry?" the cop asked me.

"Didn't want her watching television," I panted.

"Hell, the captain took care of that twenty minutes ago. He went in and pulled the plug on her set." He rubbed his jaw and frowned. "The show's all that bad?"

"Just didn't want her getting excited."

"Nothing should bother her. Her doctor sedated her an hour ago. She just had a couple of orderlies in checking on her."

"For what?"

"Beats me."

"You know them?"

"I think I've seen them around. They had their ID badges on anyway."

I said, "Damn," and went through the door. The same night-light was on and she was still there in the shaded glow of it, her breathing soft and regular. I took her wrist, felt her pulse, then let the tension go out of my shoulders.

The nurses had combed her hair out, and makeup had erased some of the discoloration on her face. The bandage was smaller and all the beauty that was Velda was beginning to reappear. A sheet was drawn up to her chin, but it didn't hide what was under it at all. She still swelled out beautifully in all the right places.

She smiled first, then opened her eyes. "I know what you were thinking," she said. Her voice was gentle, but wavering, the sedation heavy on her.

"You ought to. That's the way I always think."

"What are you doing here . . . so late?"

"Just checking."

She closed her eyes in a drowsy fashion, then seemed to force them open. "Mike . . ."

"Yeah, doll?"

"There was . . . a doctor here."

"I know . . . Burke Reedey. He gave you a sedative."

Her head rolled slightly on the pillow. "No . . . another doctor."

"An orderly?"

"He . . . looked like . . . a doctor. He said . . ." Her eyes drifted shut again.

"What did he say, honey?" I took her hand and squeezed it.

Sleepily, her eyes opened again. "He was going to . . . give me . . . another shot."

My hands suddenly went clammy. "What!"

Once again, she shook her head. "He didn't . . . do it." Her lids started to close again, then jerked open. "He told me it would make . . . me sleep better . . . and he took . . . my arm . . . when the other doctor came in."

"Another orderly?"

"Like . . . a doctor. Maybe. That first one . . . said something and . . . and left."

I said, "Son of a bitch!" and tried to let her hand go, but her fingers had a determined grip.

"Mike . . ."

I stopped trying to ease her fingers loose and looked at her. She was fighting to talk through the sedative and everything was wearing her out.

"When he spoke"—her eyelids wavered—"he sounded like . . . the one on the phone . . . Saturday . . . who wanted to meet you . . . at the office."

He was here. The lousy bastard was here in the hospital and was making a run on Velda.

I dropped her hand, patted her cheek gently and, when her eyes closed, I ducked through the door. The big cop looked at me quizzically and I nodded an okay, then asked him, "Describe that first orderly who went in there."

"Big guy, real heavyset," he said. "About five-eleven, two hundred forty pounds, dark hair going gray, Vandyke beard and mustache. Real doctor stuff. Almost like a black-and-white movie caricature."

"You said you saw him before."

"I did. I've been thinking about that. He went by here twice in the past couple of days."

"He say anything?"

"No. He just went by. The first time he was pushing a cart of surgical instruments."

"How about that second orderly?"

The cop knew something was going down and he had an anxious expression on his face. "Hell, man, he's over at the nurse's desk right now." He pointed toward the middle of the corridor and I didn't wait to hear any more.

His name was David Clinton, address on the West Side. He had been an employee of the hospital for three years, which the head nurse documented. I gave him back his ID card and took him away from the desk.

"The police officer told me you checked the lady's room tonight."

"That's right. I clean up, make sure nothing is left on the table, the lavatory is serviced . . ."

I didn't let him finish. "There was another orderly in there tonight too."

"Oh, him. That jerko was on the wrong floor. Imagine that. Those new people don't even know which button to push on the elevator."

"You report him?"

"For being on the wrong floor?"

"Never mind. Had you seen the guy before?"

He shrugged and spread his hands apart. "Well . . . I don't think so. But people come and go . . ."

"With Vandyke beards and real doctor faces?"

"I must admit, he *did* have a look about him . . . but no, I never saw him before."

There are times you want to spit and your mouth goes dry and this was one of those times. I went back to the desk, picked up the phone and got security. I gave a description of the guy to the officer in charge downstairs and told him to cover all exits. If the Vandyke crap was a disguise, he'd be big enough to recognize by height and weight.

One more call and a small argument got the operator to put a call in for Pat on the PA system. A minute later there was a click and he said, "Chambers here."

"Mike, pal. Where are you?"

"At the main desk downstairs waiting for you to come in. Where the hell have you been?"

"Hang on. I'll tell you in a minute."

The elevator took me down to the foyer and when I stepped out I saw Pat in a three-way conversation with Burke Reedey and Bennett Bradley.

I waved to the group, then pointed at Pat and motioned for him to get over to me. Quickly, I told him what had happened and said to be easy, I had alerted hospital security and Velda was all right.

"You sure?"

"Positive. The sedation might have slowed her down, but she recognized the voice. She didn't identify the face, but by damn, if Velda laid an ID on the voice it's good enough for me."

"But why go for her, Mike?"

"We got a fast-thinking killer, that's why. He tried whacking her out the first time so there would be nobody to identify him, and even if he did get a good shot at her, there's a probability she could make an identification, and that probability he can't take a chance on."

"That's what Bradley said," Pat told me. "He made an appointment to meet Burke here tonight and possibly talk to her, but your doctor buddy had already given her the sedative and didn't think it advisable."

"Nobody told me about that."

"Relax. Bradley spoke to me this evening and I told him to speak to Burke. Your girl's okay, pal. She never saw the show, she won't think the smartasses nailed you . . ."

"Then get some of your guys to cover this place. Hospital security—"

"Relax," Pat said again. "Most of the security here are retired NYPD guys." He went over to the phone, made two calls and came back. "Any more orders?"

I shook my head.

"What a pisser you are. With a time lapse like that, don't you think the guy would have been out of here? What kind of pussy you think we're dealing with?"

Burke and Bennett Bradley had been watching us curiously, so we cut it short and walked over to the desk. Burke said, "What's with you two?"

I told them what had gone on upstairs and Bradley's face went tight, his eyes drawing almost closed, and he breathed out the word "Penta" like he was saying "shit" in a foreign language.

All I could think of was that I had heard enough of Penta for a lifetime. It was a damned red-herring myth screwing up the works and nobody wanted to listen to me at all. I was the one it all started over, just me and Anthony DiCica, and now everything gets woven into a fairy-tale spider-web.

I said, "Bradley, don't give me this Penta bull-shit. You got no prints, no witnesses, no motive . . . you don't have a damn thing to bring this Penta into this except a fucking stupid note that was left on my desk beside a mutilated corpse."

He let the hardness out of his face, grimaced gently and said, "Put it this way ... we're all looking for a killer."

"He almost did it again," I said. "Velda might possibly identify his voice, but that's not hard evidence. If we could nail him with a voiceprint on tape, that's another story."

"You have a tape to match it?" Burke asked.

"We're not sure," Pat said.

"I wish somebody would be sure of something," Bradley told us. "I'd like the years I've spent following this Penta to come to something. A punctured career is no way to leave the service." He looked at the date on his watch, holding it up close so he could read the miniature letters. "I have one more week before my replacement takes over." He dropped his arm. "But it has been an exciting life, gentlemen."

Burke said, "I'll be here at eight A.M., Mr. Bradley. She should be alert enough to talk to and maybe the both of us can get her to remember something. That all right with you, Captain?"

Pat glanced at me for confirmation and I nodded. "Do what you want. I don't think you'll get anywhere, but it won't hurt trying."

"We'll go easy on her," Burke told me.

A tall, slim guy in a hospital security uniform turned the corner and walked up to Pat. Until he got close you wouldn't think he was over forty, but this one had all the markings of an old street cop and he sure knew Pat all right. He knew me too, but I couldn't place him. His men had covered the exits, checked out the premises and questioned people on every floor, but there was no sign of anybody to answer the description of the guy in Velda's room. Pat thanked him, gave me a resigned look and I put on my hat.

Pat said, "You want a lift?"

"No ... I'm going to my office and get the directions to our old buddy's place. I'll see you when I get back."

"When you going out?"

"First thing in the morning."

I said so long to everybody there and got a cab that was just pulling up to the door. The rain had let up, but the sky was rumbling away and at irregular intervals the overcast would brighten momentarily with a hidden lightning stroke inside the clouds.

The cabbie bobbed his head when I gave him my office address and we went down the drive past the row of cars that were packed bumper-to-bumper again. I looked at the place where the black Mercedes with one taillight out had been parked. This time there was a white Thunderbird and it was jammed in too tightly to go anywhere.

9

For fifteen minutes I had been poking through my desk and the assorted boxes on the shelves looking for General Rudy Skubal's address. I found everything I didn't need, but not the single sheet of a loose-leaf notepad I remembered writing it down on. My filing habits were strictly garbage-style, and if I had given it to Velda in the beginning I would have had it by now. I kicked the bottom drawer shut with my foot and sat on the edge of my chair feeling like a damn idiot.

Sometimes . . . sometimes without being asked, Velda would put things away she thought I might have use for. A piece of folded-over paper would be too much to ask for, but I gave it a try anyway.

I went outside to her filing cabinet, pulled out the drawer marked S and thumbed through the bank of folders.

And there it was, single folder, SKUBAL, RUDOLPH, GENERAL. Inside a single piece of unfolded paper from a loose-leaf notepad with directions to the old mansion on Long Island where the powerhouse from the old, wild days was kept like an aged lion, regal, but raggedy from conflict, scarred, worn and with too many years for head-to-head fieldwork. Here was where he was putting together a lifetime of notes, cryptic data now unclassified that would turn out to be the manual of manuals for covert espionage or the hairiest piece of fiction ever.

It had been a long time since I had seen him.

I was hoping he was still alive.

When I went back to the outer office I stood there a minute. The cleaners had gone over the area, the rug had been replaced, but there was still that almost imperceptible smell of Velda there. For a single second my mind flashed to the crumpled, smashed heap the killer had left her in and I knew the explosion was coming on unless I forgot about it.

One by one, I let my fists unclench, the tautness go out of my shoulders and my breathing slow down. When I was okay I locked up the office and took the elevator down. It stopped two floors below mine, and Ed Hawkins, who likes to work all night, got on with his usual two briefcases, said hello and started complaining about business. This week was bad. He barely doubled his quota and that big million wasn't coming in fast enough.

Together we walked through the foyer, signed out with the guard at the desk and pushed through the doors. We were heading in opposite directions, said so long when I saw a car break away from the curb with a wild swerve, straighten up and lay on speed. The driver's window was down, and there was a pro sitting there bringing up an Uzi automatic in his left hand to squeeze off an unimpeded burst of incredibly rapid fire.

Motion seemed to be slowed down. I was yelling, falling and grabbing at Ed's jacket all at once, then he was twisting in the air as the muzzle of the Uzi came alive with a string of unmuffled fire that sprayed bullets directly over our heads. My action had blown the gunman's rhythm and the speed of the car took him past us, and while the glass was still falling out of the doors behind us, it was all over. The car squealed around the corner and was gone.

Ed was on his face, eyes staring in terror, papers from one briefcase spilled out around him. I said, "You all right?"

He turned his head, still bug-eyed, and said, "I don't feel anything."

"You hurt?"

"No." He moved a little, his arms, then his legs. "I think I'm all right." He sat up and grinned foolishly, turned and saw the shattered doors in the office and said soberly, "Why would anybody want to kill me?"

Before I could answer, the guard came out, his service revolver in his fist. He made sure we were both unhurt, then got back to the phone and called the police. I got Ed back inside, sat him down at the desk, gave him a glass of water and grabbed the phone as soon as the guard put it down.

By now Pat would be on the way home and there was no use getting him in on this. I dialed Candace's home number, let it ring half a dozen times, then an obviously sleepy voice said, "Yes?"

I didn't want to risk an irate cut-off, so I threw it at her fast. "This is Mike, kid. Somebody just tried to hit me here at my office. It was nicely set up, an Uzi from the car window and he almost got two of us."

Suddenly the voice wasn't tired any more. "You are . . . uninjured?"

"Only my vanity was hurt. Damn, everybody wants me dead."

"Where are you?"

I gave her the address.

"Have you called the police?"

"Squad cars are on the way."

"You stay right there. I have to see you."

"Hell, I'll give my statement to the cops when they get here. I just wanted you to know this thing is coming to a fucking head."

"Stop swearing. And stay there."

This was one night the cars were in the area. The cops from two cruisers came in, visually checking the area, then came directly to the desk. I went through the ID bit again, gave them the details that were confirmed by the guard and the shaken Hawkins. There would be a followup of detectives coming by at any second and I was hoping Candace Amory got there first to keep the pressure down.

She did. She came in with a white trenchcoat thrown over a powder blue jogging suit and nobody had to tell the cops who she was. The detectives were right behind her wondering what the hell was going on, but the Icicle Lady got them all squared away in a hurry. I knew the plainclothes guys and they were giving me those strange looks that guys who have an in with girls get. She caught it too, and just let it pass.

Somehow, most of the activity had bypassed Ed and when his nerves were back on straight, he finally stood up and looked at me like Jackie Gleason's Poor Soul character and said, "They didn't want to kill me at all."

Nobody said anything.

"They were trying to kill . . . *you*, Mike."

"Yeah, I know."

"Nothing ever happens to me," he said dejectedly.

"Enjoy your near miss," I told him.

He packed the rest of his papers in his case,

nodded good night and made his way to the door, stepping over the neat piles of glass the janitor was sweeping up.

Candace had a magic way of clearing the aisles for us. There were no more questions and I knew the back way out to get around the reporters and the pair from the TV news broadcast. I wondered if that pair ever slept. Candace picked me up on the opposite street where the garage exit was and I climbed in.

I asked her, "Where to now?"

"It may sound silly, but your place or mine?"

"Let's go to yours."

"Why?"

"Because I can get out of yours."

Once again, I got that inquiring sideways look.

"It's hard to be a nice guy and get a broad out of your apartment," I explained.

"Talk about macho," she said.

"Let's talk about now. They're coming down on my head like a ton of bricks. This being-a-target shit is for the birds."

"Stop the nasty talk."

"I've heard you cut loose. Just get yourself shot at and see what you say then."

"All right. What about tonight? Who knew you'd be at your office?"

"I said it loud enough at the hospital. I was talking to Pat, but ten other people would have heard me. But that doesn't matter ... my place had been staked out. That car was waiting there.

Hell, if the mob guys want my ass, they could keep a dozen guys placed for a hit."

"They told me about the attempted mugging."

"Sure, that was for getting wise with one of the big boys. They don't like that attitude. I guess they didn't like what I did to their goons any better. By now they think it's time to go all the way."

I sat back in the seat, mulling it over again. She reached her building, let the doorman park the car for her, and we went up to her apartment. She flipped on four locks and a chain, threw her trenchcoat over a chair and went to the bar and made a pair of drinks. All the activity seemed to have run up some static electricity and the power blue jogging suit clung to her like Saran Wrap. Now she looked like a blue nude.

When she handed me the drink she motioned for me to come over to the desk. There was a sheet of paper there with the city letterhead. It was full of numbers, ending in a nine-digit figure. She put her finger under the $905 million total and said, "That's what they want to kill you for, Mike."

I put the drink down without tasting it.

"You were right. It all went back to DiCica, straight back to when he shot those two gang leaders and picked up that envelope."

"And you know what's in it?"

"Yes. Directions."

"To what?" I picked up my drink and finished

half of it. I was beginning to feel that I was going to need a boost.

Unconsciously, she flicked on the record player and the opening movement of Franz Liszt's Dante Symphony flowed out of the speakers. If she wanted suitable background music, she was going to get it.

"When does a rumor become fact, Mike?" Her voice was thoughtful.

I could have answered, but it was her show and I let her play it out.

"The officers your friend had assist me knew what they were doing. They didn't even bother assembling data or gathering evidence. All they did was have me talk to a half dozen people. Strange people. Workmen in the underworld. Everyone had the same thing to say, more or less. Do you know what the cocaine consumption in the US is?"

"I can give you the latest estimate," I told her, "and that's probably five thousand percent too low."

"Why?"

"Because interception accounts for only five percent of the narcotics trade. The suppliers have an insatiable demand to fill. Hell, they'll put up twenty percent of volume to keep the narcs away from their main shipments. Our guys used to throw a party when they grabbed a few kilos of H, and now that's real low-volume stuff. The coke coming in now runs in tons. Can you imagine that? Tons of pure shit . . . and translated to street money, it can pay off our national debt."

Liszt was getting heavy now, gently thunderous.

She turned, faced me, her eyes watching me. "Twenty years ago we never thought of deliveries in tonnage. It seemed almost impossible. There wasn't the manpower to enforce action against anything that large. The street dealers at that time weren't even set up to handle a quantity like that. Money wasn't available, the farmers, the initial producers weren't organized to grow a crop that size. Right?"

I nodded.

"Wrong," she said. "That cartel was way ahead of us. The farmers *were* producing, the laboratories were set up and while nobody thought it possible, those cocaine exporters were ready to unload on us and they made the contacts with the East Coast families to get in on the deal at a beautiful price."

Now I remembered hearing about that years ago. It was a rumor then and it was a rumor now.

She went on: "Remember, this is street talk. It's been around a long time and could have escalated with the telling."

"I know," I said.

"The cartel made the proposition through Juan Torres. The families got together, checked it out, pooled their money and bought a tractor-trailer solidly loaded with the purest cocaine you could find."

Just the thought of that much stuff hitting the street made me want to vomit. "You realize the money involved here?"

"Certainly, but imagine what it would be on the retail end when it's cut down."

"Someplace a lot of hundred-dollar bills changed hands," I said.

"They store it in temperature- and humidity-controlled bins now," she told me. "Their banking systems equal anything in Geneva, Switzerland. The cartel was given the key to the money and they gave the directions to the trailerload of coke to the organization's representatives. When DiCica killed them and picked up that envelope he turned the whole deal upside down. He held nearly a billion-dollar shipment in his hands. No way the cartel would deliver a duplicate set. Their end of the deal was over. From here on in the organization handled it themselves."

"That's some some rumor," I said. "Why did they let Torres keep operating?"

"No way Torres could have bucked the organization. He *could* have had the shipment, but not for long. The other side had all the guns."

I rattled the ice around in my glass, then drank it down. "So it was DiCica all the way, huh?"

"All the way. A stupid man who did a stupid thing. He knew where the trailer was. When they finally found him they were supposed to take him somewhere where they could squeeze the information out of him the hard way. They have some interesting ways of extracting information. The trouble was, he put up one hell of a fight and one of his attackers leaned on him a little too hard with that pipe. The fight was interrupted by a police cruiser so they didn't drag him off, but the trauma from the pipe took him out of action very effectively." She paused and took a deep breath. "I wonder what he would have done with all that cocaine?"

"He would have used it for one hell of a big bargaining chip, that's what. Even the mob would have cut a clean deal with him and let it go at that. Our own government would even set him up for life under an assumed identity to get their mitts on that load."

For one second her back went up and she started an angry denial.

I held up my hand. "Smarten up, lady. We have people in politics as dirty as those on the other side."

"Well," she told me, her face still tight, "he *really* paid for that mistake in your office."

"You know," I said, "you're back to me again. It always comes back to me. With the kind of money going down on this project, somebody *could* afford to call in an outsider like Penta to nail my ass . . . but that leaves one fucking, excuse me, big hole in the picture."

"Like what?"

"Who the hell needed him? We have pro hitters in this country."

She seemed to look at me for an eternity. "He said you killed him, Mike. What was he talking about? Could that note really have been for DiCia?"

"All I know, baby, is that it wasn't meant for me."

"It isn't over, you know." She finished her drink too and set the glass down beside mine. The first side of the Dante Symphony slid to a close and the machine flipped the record over. Now the real meat of Liszt's symphony would begin to show. "What are you going to do?"

"What I started out to do," I said. "That one son of a bitch is going to fall. I don't give a damn what happens to all the money or all the coke as long as I get that bastard under my gun. We're playing around with somebody who likes to kill, likes to get paid for killing and likes to sign his name in chopped-off fingers."

Coolly, she said, "One of you is going to find the other, Mike."

This time I grinned. "Has to happen. But before it does, sugar, I'm going to make sure you have your truckload of nose candy. When you do, you're going to let Petey Benson in on the story, lay some credit on Ray Wilson and his espionage system, then you can hop into your boss's chair and be on your way to the White House."

The beautiful blue icicle moved toward me and the static fire in the jumpsuit crackled minutely, and when her body touched mine, I felt shock that jumped from her nipple tingle in my chest, and whatever that charge did to her melted the ice completely and her mouth was on mine, eating at me, swirling and tasting, trying to vulcanize us together.

For a second I tried to hold her away, but her arms were around me and she was melting into me again. I let my fingers run down her back, following the muscles that moved along her spine, then my hands were at her waist and I knew what she wanted. I didn't do it, so she did it herself, sweeping the top of her jumpsuit off in a fast, fluid motion, and deliberately letting me have a long look at the lovely swell of those firm breasts before she pushed my coat off my shoulders and laid her breasts against my shirt so I could feel the heat, the incredible body warmth of her nakedness.

She started to smile, an impish quirk of her mouth. "Can you take off your gun?"

I unsnapped the belt loop, pulled the shoulder strap off and laid the rig on the chair. "A man's gotta do what he's gotta do," I told her.

"John Wayne said that," she mentioned.

"Many times, in many pictures."

"Now you do what *you* gotta do," she directed.

The Dante Symphony was coming to the end now. It was pounding, forcing the notes into an eerie crescendo so that you could see the flames, feel the passion and hear screams like none other anywhere. It was exhilarating to the point of absolute exhaustion and left you shaken with tremors that never came any other way.

Traffic was light going out of town. I picked up the Long Island Expressway, stayed at speed limit and let my mind wander back to when General Rudy Skubal was the main man in covert activities. During World War II he had his own unit, working under the Office of Strategic Services, and had been reassigned after the Nazi collapse to nailing war criminals trying to get out of Allied control.

He took a discharge in 1949, but the CIA was waiting then. The big action was tuning up in the cold war and it got hotter when Korea and Vietnam made their imprints on modern history. It was when the Middle East took on its own dramatic stance and developed terrorism to a high point of sophistication that the general's expertise was called on.

Then, suddenly, Rudy Skubal wasn't there any more. Somebody else occupied his office and the carefully couched words were that he had decided to retire. In a pig's ass he had *decided* to retire. He had rubbed some politico's feathers the wrong way and the power of the party had gone to work and squeezed out a real top gun and threw in some insipid party hack instead.

But old Skube didn't make any waves. He didn't have to. From then on he just made them pay for his services and kept himself the hell out of harm's way. Any more medals he didn't need.

I wondered what kind of light he was going to throw on Bern and Fells. Until now, I had never heard of any of his tigers going sour. But there always had to be a first time.

At Number 67 turnoff I picked up Route 21 North, ran past the little town of Yaphank and looked for the posts that marked the entrance to the old Kimball estate. It took thirty minutes searching and backtracking before I recognized them under a covering of wisteria, surrounded by sumac bushes. Unless the road was used almost daily, the ground covering obscured the tire tracks. I made a hard turn off the road, bounced over the culvert and felt a little relief when I knew the ground under the wheels was hard and firm.

After the first turn I was in another world. The seemingly uncared-for roughage of the exterior became a carefully tended wildlife area that quicky ended at a vast lawn surrounding a brick mansion right out of the Roaring Twenties.

Even now the general was taking no chances. Any invasion of his privacy could be clearly seen from any angle of the house, and the floodlights that were spotted around the building could turn night into day instantly.

I stayed on the driveway, going slowly, making the two large S-turns that gave the residents extra time to survey their guests, then drew up under the portico and got out of the car.

Maybe I should have called ahead. Nobody came out to meet me.

Then again, this wasn't the 1920s and the years of servants and butlers.

I walked up the stairs to the huge main door, pushed the button and heard a plain old-fashioned doorbell ring inside and then somebody appeared.

Some women can hit you with a visual impact you'll never forget. There aren't many of them, but there don't have to be many to leave a trail of men whose minds will always be impressed by a single contact. They don't have to be beautiful in any special sense, or with bodies specifically tuned to certain concepts, but to each viewer, they *are* the total thing that makes them *woman*.

This one had crazy electric blue eyes that could smile, as well as a full-lipped mouth, and when she said "Good morning," it was like being licked by a soft, satin-furry llama.

She had on a suit. The shoulders were broad, but not with the padding that was in style in 1988. She was real under the jacket and the military cut. It was tailored around beautifully full breasts, but short enough to show the generous swell of her hips. And she had a dancer's legs, muscularly rounded, but perfectly curved. They hardly make them like that any more, I thought. What she's doing here has to be a story by itself.

I said, "Damn!" under my breath and grinned back at her. "My name is Michael Hammer, ma'am. I'm an old friend of the general and I have something very important to see him about, and I'm hoping he'll have time to hear me out." I held out my wallet with the PI license and gun permit behind the plastic windows, wondering where the hell my city *schmarts* had disappeared to.

She let out a disconcerting laugh. "Well, Mr. Hammer, it *is* nice to see you. Please, come in."

"Thanks." I stepped up and walked past her. She was another big woman, with elfish grace, yet strangely athletic motion. She closed the door with a sweep of her hand, then thumbed open a panel and touched a red lighted button that went out momentarily and turned green.

"May I have your weapon?" she asked me.

I flipped out the .45 and handed it to her. She took it, slipped it inside a small wall closet and covered that too. "You didn't ask me for a throw-away piece." I said.

"That's because you haven't any." She smiled back. "Keys, pocket change and possibly a pen-knife, but nothing more. The instrument is very sensitive."

"Supposing somebody just comes busting in here—"

"Why talk of unpleasant things?" she said. "Now, I haven't introduced myself. I am Edwina West, General Skubal's secretary."

"Hold it."

She paused. "Mr. Hammer?"

"Let's keep it simple and square, Miss West. No secretary garbage."

"Oh?"

"You're CIA, aren't you?"

There was no hesitation at all. "Yes, I am. Why should you ask?"

"Women don't generally refer to a gun as a weapon. You knew what a throwaway was."

Her smile had real laughter in it. "I'll have to remember that," she told me. "Do you like me any less now?"

It was my turn to laugh. "You're some kind of doll, Miss West. You make a guy feel like he walked into a propeller."

"Please, call me Edwina."

"Okay, Edwina. Just tell me . . . is it genetic?"

She took my arm and folded it around her own. "My mother seemed to have some sort of attraction for men too. Don't all women have that?"

"Honey, not the way you have it. You must have been a terror when you were growing up."

"Do you know how old I am, Mr. Hammer?"

"Mike," I told her. "And I'd say you were forty, forty-two." Usually, when you lay that on a beautiful woman you feel the chill. A cold can come off them like a shore-bound fog and you get the thrust of mental death.

But not her. She said, "I am forty-eight. Does that disappoint you?"

I said, "Watch it, Edwina, you're touching nerves I didn't know I had."

She squeezed my arm with her fingers. It was a long, gentle, but soft grasp and she said, "Don't be surprised at what I know about you. I've read the profile the general has on you, the accounts the press have touched on and a lot of information you probably consider extremely personal."

I stopped, turned us around and looked at the door forty feet behind us. We were in a big foyer, a generous room lined with expensive fixtures I hadn't noticed until now. I said, "Kid, we just met, we walked about thirteen yards together and I could write a book about what's happened inside three minutes. Does that happen all the time?"

The way her mouth worked when it was starting to smile was startling. Those incredibly blue eyes were almost hypnotic. "Only when I want it to," she said. "And there is something else."

"What's that?"

She turned me around toward a pair of heavy hand-carved oaken doors, tugged very easily on an ornate brass handle and the door opened noiselessly and without effort. "*That* I will tell you later."

The house was real enough, the kind you could get lost in, the kind they used for background in period motion pictures, or classic horror films.

Edwina gave me a small tour on the way to see the general, but everything got lost in the throaty rich tone of her voice. There was music in it, low and demanding. There was a light touch of lust and overtones I could feel, but couldn't describe, and when we got to the final door I began to wonder what the hell had happened to me. I was in some kid's damn daydream acting like I had my head up my ass and enjoyed it. I finally let out a laugh and she knew I was laughing at myself, gave me one of those lovely grins back and knocked on the door.

A buzzer clicked and the door swung open. We stepped inside and the door closed automatically.

A light was on us, so bright it cut off all vision of anything behind it like a solid wall.

I heard a chuckle, and a voice that hadn't changed at all with the years said, "Good afternoon, Michael."

The light went off with a metallic *ping* and another came on that lit up the office. Back there at the same old desk, but now surrounded by rows and banks of electronic equipment, was General Rudy Skubal.

I said, "Hello, General."

"What do you think?"

"Pretty damn dramatic," I told him.

"You're only looking at the surface." He waved at us. "Come on over here." He pushed himself out of his chair and held out his hand. I took it, enjoying the good grip the old man still had. "How long has it been, Michael?"

Hell, he would have known to the day, but I said, "Many moons, General. You still look pretty sharp."

"Eyewash. I'm becoming enfeebled. It's a pain in the butt, yet unavoidable." He tapped the side of his head. "Up here I can go on indefinitely, and with the machines much can be accomplished, but the old physical thrill of the chase is gone. I haven't popped anybody in the teeth in so long I hardly remember what it sounded like."

"It never sounds," I said. "They break off quietly. If you cut your hand on them, you can get one hell of an infection."

General Skubal squinched up his face and shook his head angrily. "Hell, man, you see that? You remember? Damn, you still get to do those things and have the fun. *You* kick ass and get laid and I push buttons."

"Don't sweat it, General. It's only fun when you live to remember it," I reminded him, "and with the security you have here you'll live long enough."

He ran his fingers through his mop of blazing white hair and let me see a small smile. "Don't overrate Edwina here. She causes me more anxious moments than the enemy. You know she's CIA, don't you?"

"Of course."

"You tell him?" he asked her.

"No, he knew," she answered.

"See, that's why I wanted to recruit this guy," he said. "What an agent he would have made." He paused, looked at the both of us a second, a wrinkle showing in his forehead. "He would have straightened you out, gal."

She looked straight at me, a bright blue stare daring me to say it. So I said it. "General, you *never* straighten out lovely curves like that."

I watched old Skubie frown again and look up at me from under his whiskery eyebrows. Finally he said, "Edwina, go rassle us some coffee and Danish, okay?"

She winked at us both, waited for the general to trip the door buzzer and left. "Crazy," I said.

"I never had that when I was young," the general muttered. "Now, Michael, I assume this is not a 'just happened to be in the neighborhood' call."

"Pure business, General."

"Our kind of business?"

"Right."

He flipped a set of switches on a control panel in front of him, then leaned back in his chair, his hands folded behind his head. "One more assumption . . . this has to do with the death in your office?"

The old guy was on the ball all right. "That's how it started."

"Okay, shoot," he said. "Tell it your own way."

I gave it to him in detail the way it opened up,

setting the stage with the way I found Velda and the mutilated body of DiCica in my office. He knew about the note, but when I mentioned the name Penta, his lips pursed, he took his hands down and wrote out the name on a pad, then sat back and listened again. I ran the whole thing down for him without bothering to tail off into DiCica's initial role. Anything he could give me I wanted to point directly at the killer himself.

Halfway through, the buzzer sounded. Edwina came in with the coffee and Danish, put them down on the desk and went back out again. When we stirred the coffee up, the general nodded for me to continue.

I took him through the details Russell Graves had dug up, the data Ray Wilson had brought out of the computers and the events that led to Harry Bern and Gary Fells being mentioned as cadets the general had in his old unit.

When I finished, the general leaned on the desk and touched his fingertips together. "You're stirring up old memories, Michael. The names you mentioned, I know those people well. Carmody has always been a good career man. If you remember, he was the one who grabbed that bunch hijacking trucks last year. Ferguson spent his early years in the European sector. Speaks four languages, I understand. The last administration brought him to this area. Bennett Bradley was always a good man for State. He had the makings of an operative, you know, but too conservative.

His forte, as I remember it, was political science. Too bad they're forcing retirement on him." He stood up, pushing his chair back. "However, before we get to Bern and Fells, let me have a brief consultation." He nodded toward a computer bank. "Want to watch?"

"Sure," I said. "Why not?"

This was the new battlefield now. Nothing dirty, no wild screams of terror or staccato noises of fast-firing guns. No sliding around in muck or taking high dives onto hard flats to get out of a field of crossfiring rifles. No knives or insidious poisons or wire garrotes nearly decapitating a human. Now it was quiet button-tapping sounds and lighted letters and numbers flashing on the screen, being rearranged, rechanneled for new information, positioning themselves into faraway circuits, then returning in seconds.

The general had entered his request for knowledge of the one called Penta. It was caught up in the wizardry of electronics and General Skubal sat back and let the machine take over. While it worked, he said to me, "In case you're interested . . ."

"General, I'm *very* interested."

"My so-called retirement was not for very long. The idiots who pulled me were dumped at the next election and I was reinstated right where I wanted to be . . . here, and at government expense. These machines are owned and serviced by federal funds and are state-of-the-art equipment. And believe me," he added, "the government is getting their money's worth . . . and I'm living doing what I can do best."

"Tell me, General, how secure are you here?" I looked around at the enormity of the project, knowing that this was the best of miniaturization.

He said, "There are eighty people billeted here. That placid landscape you saw outside is one huge deathtrap of a minefield, each charge being detonated electrically from inside here, or isolated to operate independently. With the electronic sensors we use, no dogs are necessary, no patrols needed, so we look indeed like a quiet retreat in the country."

"How about power?"

"There's a solar collector on the roof. Storage batteries can last two weeks at full power. Of course, this is in addition to regular power supplied by underground cable. Beneath the building is a deep well with reserves for fire-fighting supplies. Our food larder can last a month and if you're a drinking man, those needs are supplied too."

"That's a siege condition, General."

"Yes. But these days, you never know, do you? At least this is what we're protecting." His hand indicated his vast electronic battlefield.

Then the face of the screen that was blank lit up. The name Penta appeared, then the sketch story about the one who appeared as a will-o'-the-wisp on the world scene.

Penta meant nothing. It was a code name assigned by the CIA. There was no physical description. Penta's activities had been linked with the Stern Gang and the Red Brigade. His terrorist actions were noted by certain dictatorship governments, and it is suspected that he often worked on their behalf. Sixteen known assassinations were attributed to him, all of them with various forms of digital butchery done to the victims.

I said, "Digital butchery?"

"Newspeak for finger-chopping."

"Great."

"Interesting note here ... Penta is suspected of being a mole in the NATO organization. He had to have inside information to accomplish several of his kills. No proof offered, but circumstantial evidence is hard. Now look at this."

Three CIA reports came on-screen with information compiled by Bennett Bradley. Twice he had almost cornered Penta when national police action of one foreign country stymied his move. The third time he was shot in the thigh by Penta and his quarry got away. There was a fourth item suggesting Bradley be removed from the assignment. Now I could understand his last-ditch attitude, wanting to grab Penta before his replacement got into the act.

The words stopped appearing. Two lines of dots went across the screen, then five groups of letters, six letters to a set, appeared, the last group flashing on and off regularly. The general grunted, took a key from his pocket and walked to a safe against the wall. He spun the dial three times, opened the thick door, then used the key on a box inside.

"What are the letters in the last group?" he called out.

"*R T V W Y*," I called back.

He closed the box, put it back and slammed the safe shut. When he sat down again he punched a key and the screen went blank. "This Penta person is over here on one hell of a high-level assignment."

"To kill me, General?" Damn, it was starting again, right here.

"You worth killing?"

"Not to anybody I know."

"How about to somebody you don't know?"

I sat down and my teeth were grinding together. I took a couple of breaths, relaxed and looked at the old guy. There was knowledge and patience and wisdom sitting there, and somehow he knew what I was thinking and was trying to direct my own thoughts in a logical direction.

This was one direction that didn't allow for logic. I shook my head. "No way. You can't go through me and locate Penta. The road to that guy is through Bern and Fells. That's the connection. Those two are looking for Penta and if we can run them down, we can get inside the reasoning behind all this. There's a motive, General. It's good enough to kill and destroy for and when we have that, we have Penta."

"I can give you Fells and Bern," he said simply. "You familiar with their history?"

"Somewhat."

"Wild ducks, that pair. Unstable, adventuresome ... after they left the service, they laid down a pretty greasy trail. Three different countries hired them for covert work and they did a damn good job for them. Libya was their last employer."

He wasn't finished and I didn't push him. "The last three jobs attributed to Penta—political assassinations of top personnel—were at the behest of some Arab organization inside Libya."

"So the three were contemporaries in possibly related actions."

"Possibly."

"And now Penta and Fells and Bern are over here together," I said, "only now they've lost touch. Bern and Fells want to locate Penta badly. They think I have a lead and try to squeeze it out of me. Question: How did they lose track of Penta?"

"I know a better question," General Skubal told me. "Why were they looking for him in the first place? Penta is *not* an organization man. Penta is a loner, a total loner absolutely dedicated to his work."

"Let's go a step further, General," I suggested. "He is here, so his work is here. His targets never were minimal, so his target *now* isn't minimal, and so far he hasn't nailed his intended target." I saw the way he was looking at me and added, "Forget the crap about him going for me."

"Who shot at you, Michael?"

I didn't say anything.

"Okay, you have another angle too. I suspected that."

"I only want Penta. After what he did to Velda, he is mine. Just mine. What else he's here for won't matter. When I meet him, everything else gets wiped out along with him and it will all be over. Now tell me about Fells and Bern."

The general poured himself another cup of coffee and popped in a few cubes of sugar. "That pair are on FBI and CIA wanted lists, and that's for starters. Unfortunately, they've been too well trained for our people to put them down. So far, nobody made any inquiries to me, or I might have steered them to a few points that might bear fruit with a stakeout."

"They know they're wanted?"

"No doubt," he confirmed. "But now they're here, and there's one thing they've probably forgotten about. Like any of the people in our work, they have safe houses to hole up in right in their enemies' backyard. We establish these places for them, or when necessary they can make the arrangements themselves. Fells and Bern like to do their own work. They didn't want *anybody* knowing where they had a safe house, including me.

However, I realized that, and knowing the way their personalities were developing, I made sure I ran down the three places they had on the East Coast. They never found out and I never published the information because they were operating in Europe most of the time."

"They came back often enough."

"Sometimes it is better to watch the rats to see what's happening than kill them outright. They didn't make the high-priority wanted lists until fairly recently."

"Where are the houses, General?"

"This I don't bring up on the computers. Wait here. I want to make some phone calls."

I sat there, made another cup of coffee for myself and finished a Danish before he got back.

He sat down and looked at the piece of paper in his hand. "One was in Freeport, Long Island."

"Was?"

"It burned down a year ago. Another was in the Boston area. The city ran an expressway through the site. Forget it."

"Damn, is this going down the tubes too?" I demanded impatiently.

"The last one's in Brooklyn. Unfortunately, it's in an area slated for demolition. I have an operative checking on the situation now."

"Hell, can't we just move in and . . . ?"

"These guys aren't amateurs, Michael. They'll have everything covered. First we find out what the status is, then you can plan your move. My man is going to call back. He'll leave one word as to the situation. If he says yes, then it's a go. It's all yours, my boy. There's no help unless you ask for it and I doubt if you're going to do that."

"You doubt correctly, General. Just tell me one thing."

"What's that?"

"How come you invite me right into your super-world and let me peek at all the classified good-ies and give me such undivided attention when all I am is a plain old private-style investigator?"

"Your personal profile, my boy," he said cheer-fully. "I remember every word of it. Besides, one more after Penta can't hurt anything."

"Baloney," I said.

His cheerful smile disappeared and his face was flat. All of a sudden we were two nasties ready to go after the other nasties. "You're a damn killer, buddy," he told me. "We need peo-ple like you."

"What are my odds, General?"

"Against Fells and Bern? I'll give you the edge there. They have the training. You have the in-stinct on top of it."

"What about Penta?"

He pushed a button on the desk, waited until Edwina answered and said, "I'm going to take my nap. I want no calls and no visitors. Mr. Hammer will stay until he gets his message. Please see that he is taken care of." He wiped his eyes, moved his shoulders in a shrug, then peered up at me. *"You die for killing me,"* he said softly. "A riddle. A veritable riddle."

"All riddles get solved," I said.

When Edwina came into the room he handed her a slip of paper. "If the caller says yes, then give this to Michael here. It's an address he'll want to look into. Let's not send him on a wild goose chase if it's not necessary."

She looked at the paper, went to a small machine, dropped it into an opening and pushed a button. A puff of smoke came out. She smiled and said, "Security," holding out her hand to steer me to the doorway.

"Would you like to see the house?"

"I'd rather see the security systems."

"That's a negative, of course."

"Let me tell you something, kid. My imagination is enough to figure out everything they have laid down. Frankly, I hope it's the best. The only part I don't like is the lack of manpower on the perimeter. Some wise guy can always figure a way to interrupt any kind of electrical system."

She ran her fingers down my arm and took my hand. "That's what they have me for. I'm supposed to distract them."

We started walking toward the glass-enclosed veranda. I gave her a long, inquiring look. "That's the other thing. Just *what* is a doll like you doing here anyway? You're not a secretary."

At the door she opened the panel box and flipped a switch, then closed it. "No, not primarily."

We walked out onto the enclosed porch area and looked over the vast openness of the estate. It had a strange color of green, and I knew we were looking through one-way glass. "Don't give me the bodyguard bit. Women can be good, but the strong-arm act goes to the men."

"True," she agreed.

I dropped her hand, took her by the shoulders and kept her back to me. She tightened a little bit when I ran my hands over her, under her arms, down her sides, then felt each thigh down to her knees.

When I stood up she said, "You forgot to look for a derringer between my titties."

I did a gentle probe and said, "Satisfied?"

"How did you know?"

"You turned the alarm off, sugar. I'm clean, so that leaves you with some hidden metal that could trigger the gizmo."

"Mike, you *are* clever. No wonder the general thinks so highly of you."

"I'm curious, lady."

She smiled at me. A damp, coy smile that was a ripe invitation.

Three brass buttons held the jacket closed and my thumb flipped them loose one by one, the last one almost springing away from the pressure of her breasts. She shrugged, and her jacket fell to the floor and she put her arms around my neck, her big blue eyes full of pleasure and adventure. Inside the sheer silk blouse she flowed like honey, not needing a bra to keep her breasts high and firm.

I touched her lightly again and she knew what I was feeling for. She made a little gesture with her head and didn't try to stop me. But there were no scars from surgical implants or reconstruction work.

Around her waist she wore a three-inch-wide leather belt with ornate silver decorations in a flowing Mexican pattern. "That's what would set the alarm off," she told me.

I fingered the hand-tooled buckle anyway and tugged it loose. The belt was a beautiful piece of work, every bit of the leather touched by the artisan's hand. Even the silver was embossed with intricate design work in delicate patterns.

All but two pieces. They weren't silver. They were a dull-finish alloy and I opened the catches and took the .22-caliber shots out of the midget chambers, two little slugs that could rip far into your guts up close, enough to ring your bell for keeps.

"Cute," I said. "You *are* strong-arm after all."

"Well, I couldn't really wear a piece the size of yours, could I?"

"Why the snakey stuff, Edwina?"

"Regulations. We have to be armed at all times. The choice of weapons is at our discretion in situations like this."

"And that's what I asked you to start with. What *is* your assignment here?"

Her arms came from around my neck and she laced the fingers of her hand around mine. With her other hand she took the belt from me and dropped it on top of her jacket. "Would you believe me if I told you?"

The blue eyes were yearning, trying to say something. She wet her lips gently, and I had to stare at the slickness of her mouth. Her lips parted and I could see the pinkness of her tongue. "R and R," she said.

Rest and recreation.

"This is a hell of a place for that."

"I needed the rest. They made me take three months of it."

"But why?" I insisted.

She took her hand away, ran the zipper down on the side of her skirt and it dropped to the floor. The flimsy silken bikini bottom only enhanced what it tried to hide and when she pulled her blouse open, I saw what had happened. Her belly had been ripped by three bullets that went in the front at an angle and exited the sides through the soft flesh, and the healed pucker marks were still red and angry-looking.

"Who did that, Edwina?"

"It doesn't matter."

I nailed those blue eyes with my own. I knew my teeth were showing in a nasty grin.

"I was in the field," she said. "I wasn't careful enough."

"Anybody drop the guy?"

"No. He got away." She was looking at me carefully now. "Does it disgust you?"

I shook my head. "I got a couple myself. They're medals, kid. Treat them like medals." I put my hands on her naked waist and pulled her in close to me. "You are one special woman, Edwina. The air seems to shimmer around you. I can feel your body heat and watch you pulse with whatever's going on inside that body of yours. Those scars on you aren't ugly. They tell the world all about you. Hell, on you they even look good."

Sparkling blue. The eyes went sparkling blue and grew sleepy-lidded. I saw her mouth come close, soft and damp, and I leaned forward to meet it, and tasted the deep essence of her. For that short interval I was completely absorbed into a strange wonder, locked tightly with a naked woman on a huge windowed veranda, far away from all the wild thoughts of the past days.

Very slowly I came back to the real day and held her away from me just to look at. "All this in a few hours," I said.

"You told me something earlier, Mike. Now let me tell you. What you saw in me, I see in you."

"A crazy world, kid," I said softly.

A softly muted bell hummed behind me. Edwina turned, picked up the phone, waited a moment, then put it down again. "That was your contact."

My breath hung in my chest.

"He said yes."

I just looked at her and a little sadness came into her eyes. "R and R," she told me again. "I've had the rest, but I think the recreation is going to have to wait."

This time I hauled her into me. Not gently. She didn't need gently any more. I handled her like she needed to be handled and her mouth on mine was a firebox that moved all over me. She felt my hands on her and knew what they were saying, that there would be another time and another place because it had to happen, maybe just once, but it had to happen.

Our mouths were bruised, but it had been a happy war, and she gave me the address I wanted, got back into her clothes and led me to the huge front doors. She gave me my .45 back, closed the doors as I was going down the stairs, and I got in the car and headed back to New York.

There was no way I could make a quick pass around my block to see if I was being singled out. If somebody wanted me, they would know my car, the approaches to the apartment, and stay out of sight. Two blocks away I parked in a public area under an office building, and started walking back. The stop at the newspaper kiosk on the corner was more an excuse to take a look around than buy a copy of the *News*, but when I picked it up, I saw one of the four-color tabloids that turned a goodnight kiss into a Roman orgy, and my face and Velda's were spread right across the front of it under the masthead: PRIVATE INVES-TIGATOR TO AVENGE LOVER'S ATTACK.

Until now Velda had just been an innocent victim when the intruder came into my office. Now she was hot copy. Her name was only mentioned in the initial reports of the event, then forgotten.

I remembered the way that reporter had looked at me when I casually said what I'd like to do to DiCica's killer. He suddenly had a sex angle bigger than the murder itself and got into national circulation damn near overnight. One day I was going to meet that little sucker again, and we were going to have a nice talk in a quiet place.

When the light on the corner changed, I buried myself in a group of people, stayed with them to the garage entry of my building and turned in with a car going down the ramp to park. I knew the area down here and it was easy to make sure I was clear. I took the elevator up all alone, got out with the .45 in my hand, then put it back in the holster when I saw no one in the corridor.

10

I was sweaty from the drive and had to change clothes, pissed off at the time I'd had to waste making sure the area was clear. I took a fast shower, got dressed and called Pat. He was still at the office and barked a hello into the phone.

"It's me, buddy," I said. "I got an address for Fells and Bern. They still use an active safe house in Brooklyn."

"Mike, damn it, there's nothing we can do on that end of it."

"Then call Bradley and let him straighten it out. If the other agencies can't get close on this, they'll have to go along with us."

"This address a positive?"

"You got it."

"Where are you?"

"Home."

"Stay there. I'll buzz Bradley and call you back."

I looked at the clock. It was a quarter to nine. I walked to the desk, got the bottle of Canadian Club out and made myself a normal-size drink, splashing in the ginger ale over the ice. I turned the TV on, watched CNN for ten minutes, switched to the sports channel and finished the drink.

The phone went off. I grabbed it and Pat said, "Bradley okayed the deal. We're all meeting in my office in an hour."

"I'll be there."

"Give me that address first. No telling what can happen to you on the way over."

"Thanks," I said, and gave him the street and number.

My car I left sitting in the garage. It was easier to have the attendant flag me a cab down on the street, then hop in, covered by the parked cars on the street. Twenty minutes later I was walking into Pat's office. He had already contacted a precinct in Brooklyn and was organizing a layup for the raid.

I caught him between calls and asked, "Any problems with Bradley?"

"He sounded glad something positive was happening. He's picking up Ferguson and Frank Carmody."

"Carmody? The FBI is still holding an interest?"

"They're observers on this deal. NYPD makes the collar and they head up the interrogation, which is okay with me. You're along on this out of the goodness of our hearts and because there's no way of keeping you out of it. Keep your nose clean, will you?"

"Don't sweat me out, pal. You have the safe house staked out?"

"Nobody is getting in or out of that block until we say so. You ready to move?"

"Anytime."

Behind me Bennett Bradley came in with Ferguson and Carmody, their faces serious. Bradley was the only one not carrying, which was fine with me. Bradley tapped me on the shoulder and said, "I understand you came up with this lead."

"I lucked out."

"Who was your source?"

"Confidential, Mr. Bradley."

"I hope it pans out," he said. "How are we getting there?"

Pat slipped into his jacket and checked the .38 on his belt. "There are a couple of unmarked cruisers downstairs. Now, I'm going to run over our positions just once. Remember, you're observers. We do the active work."

He took five minutes outlining what he wanted on a green blackboard, then got us out of there.

They said Brooklyn never changes, but it does.

There was a different time, but now is now and the stupidity of progress had taken over. The neighborhoods had dissolved into complexes and the high-rises had become the crucibles of trouble, the old trying to retain what they had, the new ones caught up in the money world where all is a quick fuck, a coke high and a hole in the ground.

I thought, *A long time ago, I was born here. Menahan Street. It's buried now under a pile of rubble, reconstructed later into a sand-and-plaster heap of garbage.*

The cop said, "What's wrong, Mike?"

"I used to live here."

"When?"

"Before it changed."

"You're an old timer," he said.

"Hell, I was only a year old."

The cop grinned and went over to his station. Pat finished directing his crew and walked over to me.

"This better be good," he said, and touched the button on his flashlight.

They hit with all the precision in the world, quietly and close-shouldered. One team went in from the rear, one swarmed over the rooftop and the hot squad went right in through the front.

I sat and watched and nothing happened. They all came out, untied their bulletproof vests and when I went over to where Pat was operating the station, he put down his earphone and said, "Two dead men inside."

"Who?"

"Damned if I know. Let's go see."

And they were dead. These were the quiet dead. No big holes in them, just a fast slug into a vital part and dead. The shot was knowledgeable, direct and certain. No screams. Whatever happened to them happened so fast they only had a chance to gasp, then die.

Both of them were sitting at a table, coffee and soft rolls in front of them. Whatever hit them happened so quickly they never had a chance to react.

The killer had come in the door, shot the one who was facing him square in the forehead and the one sitting opposite in the back of the skull. The wound entries were about the size a .22 would make, but there were no exit holes and there was a strange expansive look about both the heads.

Pat looked at both the bodies carefully, a grimace drawing across his mouth. "I've seen hollow-tips do this. They fragment inside the skull and create a pressure that can make features pretty damn grotesque."

"Wasn't much of a safe house," I said.

But now the picture was a little clearer. The two dead guys had been on the prowl for Penta, all right. He was their target. This thing had all the earmarks of a contract kill that went sour.

Penta had gotten wise. Penta had gotten to them first. Someplace Penta had picked up their trail, followed them to the safe house and eliminated them. That is, if they were Bern and Fells.

Dead bodies don't take long to smell. The odor from these two was starting to bubble up and when we had enough, Pat said, "Look at their fingers."

The tips had been cut off very neatly.

I said, "Another signature."

"The one on DiCica was even better. He had a real mad on when he carved up that guy."

"Don't say it, Pat." I knew what he was thinking.

Lewis Ferguson made the identification. He came in behind us and said, "That's Bern and Fells, all right."

"They're pretty bloated," Pat said. "You'd better be sure."

"Positive. Prints will confirm it."

Pat nodded and called one of the detectives over. "Get all the preliminaries done, then sweep this place good. Like I mean take it apart. When you're done, I want it to look like the city wrecking crew was here. Pick your guys, keep the clowns out of here. I want some evidence, something, anything of what went on here. You got it?"

"Got it, Captain."

Carmody and Ferguson were having a serious conversation with Bradley when we came out.

Jurisdiction seemed to be the heart of the matter, but Pat called a halt to that in a hurry. He said, "Let's get something squared away, people. We got two more corpses inside *my* area and that's where it's going to stay. You guys can play around with any espionage or international bellyaches you want, but these bodies belong to NYPD and until I get a direct order from my superior, that's the way it goes."

"Captain . . ." Bradley started.

Pat held up his hand. "Don't challenge me, Bradley. NYPD is a bigger outfit than yours and if you want to see how clout works, just mess around with this investigation."

"No intention of doing that, Captain," Bennett Bradley said. "Let's say that all of our agencies are anxious to cooperate in any way."

Ferguson agreed. "This has overlapped into strange areas. Stumbling blocks we don't need."

One of the uniformed cops came up with a detective and got Pat's attention. The detective said, "Patrolman Carsi here was working in the back. There's a garage attached to the building."

"Not quite attached. A walkway goes into the cellar," the patrolman told him. "There's a car in there. Pretty lush."

And there was the Mercedes. The rear taillight was broken.

I said, "If you find my prints in there, you know when it happened."

There were New York State plates on the car,

but a current Florida tag was on the floor under the front seat. In the glove compartment were all the goodies belonging to a Richard Welkes with a Miami Beach address.

A uniformed sergeant drove by and told Pat that the press had just arrived on the other block. Pat muttered an annoyed "Damn," then instructed the detective with him to go rough things in for them, playing it down as much as possible. An unidentified squeal on a couple of dead bodies could command the amount of police attention that was in the area, so there shouldn't be any kickback from the news hounds. Not right now, anyway.

Within an hour only the investigative crew was left. A pair of uniforms stayed out of sight in the doorway, alert and quiet. Carmody came up with containers of coffee and we passed it around. You could hear nails being wrenched out of boards inside the building and occasionally something came crashing down.

Forty-five minutes later a dust-covered detective came to the doorway and waved to Pat. "You better come over here, Captain."

He told me, "Wait here," and followed the cop inside.

In ten minutes he came out with a small box in his hands, nodded toward the cars and said, "Let's go."

I sat beside him in the back and didn't say a word. He was waiting for me to throw a question because it was my work that had opened the murders up. Twice, in his reflection in the window, I saw him watching me.

Finally I said, "Now it jumps back into Bradley's hands, doesn't it?"

He said it very softly. "How'd you figure that out?"

"I get tingling sensations." I hit the window button and let some air in. "Why did those two want to hit Penta?"

"He wasn't doing his primary job. He was off on something else."

I looked down at the box in his lap.

"The assholes didn't destroy a letter of authorization they got. We can assume it was Penta they were after, but the person was simply mentioned as 'Subject.' "

"What was Penta's primary job, Pat?"

"You mention this to anybody and you're on my permanent shit list."

"Don't insult me, buddy."

"Sorry, Fells sent a letter to Harry Bern. He had gotten a contact from their employer overseas who wanted to know if they wanted the assignment of killing the VP."

"The *who*?"

"VP. I assume it stands for vice president."

"Of what?" I asked him.

"Let's start with the United States."

"Pat . . . why the hell would anybody want

the vice president dead? I can understand the president . . ."

"Hold it, will you? Apparently Penta screwed up someplace along the line and his employer would only tolerate one mistake. Fells and Bern were offered *his* initial contract *after* they wiped him out. If those two could take out Penta, they certainly could hit the VP."

"Somebody has a damn good reason. With the VP dead, think of the consternation it would cause in Washington. Man, they never could figure that one out. The VP doesn't get the personal coverage the president does, so he would be an easier target. But hell, that's still hitting right at the heart of our government."

"What bigger target has he got than that, for Pete's sake?"

Pat just looked at me a couple of seconds. "I can't believe it," he said.

My eyes started to go tight. "Believe what?"

"If the so-called subject *is* Penta, where *you* would come into the picture." He stopped me before I could get a word out. "I know, you're not in. He was after DiCica and all the crap. But I can't figure that way. How the hell you do it, I'll never know. I've said that before too, haven't I? How the hell you go from kicking around in the streets to substituting for the vice president of the United States in a murder scheme defies belief. Where do you come from, Mike? I've known you all these years, but I don't think I know you very well at all."

"Pat . . ."

He shook his head. "You've been running me, haven't you? Here I thought you were my boy and I was running . . . all the time you have something else going down." He paused, wiped his hand across his face and took a deep breath. "What's happening, Mike?"

I shrugged. "What else is in the box?"

"Forty-two one-thousand-dollar bills," he said.

"Be hard to cash," I told him.

"What's happening, Mike?" he asked again, ignoring my remark.

"Tomorrow, Pat. I have to make sure of something first."

"You know, I'm a lousy cop, old buddy. I have you inside this package like you're the PC or something. I have my neck out, giving you information, breaking all the rules—"

"Balls. You had no choice. Like Candace Amory said, I'm an adjunct of the law, licensed by the state, subject to conditions no ordinary citizen has to operate under. Consider it professional courtesy."

"I must be off my rocker," he said.

"You going by your office?"

"I have to."

"Good. I want to use your phone."

When we reached Pat's office I slid behind Pat's desk into his chair and punched the num-

ber into his phone. I had one foot up on Anthony
DiCica's antique toolbox, which Pat had in the
kneehole, but took it off when I realized what it
was.

She picked up the phone on the first ring and
there was no sleepiness in her voice at all. I said,
"This is Mike, Candace."

"Well, I've been waiting to hear from you."

"The grapevine working?"

"Not until after the Brooklyn soiree was over.
I understand there were two bodies found."

"Both shot."

"I don't suppose you'd care to explain further."

"Right. All information will come from official
sources. It's strictly a police matter."

She had to probe with a lawyer's instinct. "But
you were there?"

"The police acted on my information. I went
along for verification."

"Very neat."

"What's new on that load of cocaine?"

"Something extremely interesting. It's totally
hearsay, but often enough what sounds like a
fairy tale is factual. Your friend Ray Wilson came
up with another lead, an old dealer who is straight
now and doesn't want his name mentioned in
any way."

"So?"

He had heard about the shipment being set up.
It was delivered by freighter at Miami, concealed
as bags of coffee beans. The shipper was genuine

and the destination was a reputable buyer. Nobody knows just how the switch was made, but the cargo was off-loaded into a tractor-trailer."

"Do you realize how much stuff that is?"

"In dollars the final street value is incredible. Anyway, it came up via Route Ninety-five into the New York area. The trailer was delivered to a depot in Brooklyn, all the paperwork completed, and the next day another tractor signed for them, hauled them out and it hasn't been seen to this day."

"You can't just hide a trailer," I told her. "I can see the run being made, but you'd still be dealing with a driver who probably had a helper along."

"Thanks to Ray Wilson we found a possible line on that one too. He went into the computers for known mob persons who could handle trucks. Not live ones, but deceased. He came up with two names of men who were found dead in a car that had apparently been sideswiped and knocked off Route Nine-W up near Bear Mountain. Two days later the brother of one was killed in a hit-and-run accident in Newark."

"That took care of the driver and a helper," I said. "Your hearsay is making pretty good sense."

"But *somebody* would know where the cargo went to. Whoever gave the instructions to the two men DiCica killed would know."

"Sure," I said. "The driver and the helper would have known. Those guys were probably made men who would lay down their lives for their bosses. They were taking no chances on any hijack action so they planned the delivery themselves, which could have meant repainting the truck or changing the lettering somewhere along the way. The legitimate driver on the first leg of the run really took the odds for the mob boys. His making it to Brooklyn meant the job was coming out clean."

"Then the driver and helper were the only ones who knew?"

"Why not? The fewer the better. They picked their own hiding spot for the shipment, made up a map and delivered it to the bosses. On the way out they were followed by the hit men and taken out in a supposed accident."

"Why kill . . ."

"The bosses didn't want anybody but them knowing where the stuff went to," I told her. "Unfortunately, they were in line for a hit themselves that night. And unfortunately, they closed off the mob's only access to the stuff."

"And DiCica had it all."

"Wild, huh? Tell me something. How much is the street value of the junk today?"

She told me. I let out a low whistle. No wonder Penta could afford to pass up the VP for an old hood. Nine-digit figures are understandable.

YOU DIE FOR KILLING ME.

Okay, DiCica. You were the hit man. That was

your trade. Who did you kill and how did you work it? That note was for you after all, wasn't it?

"Mike . . ."

I shook myself out of my thoughts. "Sorry, kid."

"Unless we find that cargo, nothing will ever end."

"Is Ray checking out all the leads?"

"The trailer would take a certain size building to be concealed in. He's working on the assumption something was bought, rather than leased. By now taxes would be owing and if anything matches, we'll be on it."

"You don't have that much time."

"Any other options?"

"A lot of luck. We still have a killer out there waiting."

"For what?"

"Pat will have to tell you that. Or Coleman or Carmody or Ferguson."

"You going to be around?"

I told her I would. She said she'd call tomorrow and I hung up. I would have gone home and crawled into bed, but I called in to check the tapes on my phone and a deep, sultry voice said to call at any hour.

When the call went through, General Rudy Skubal answered it himself. As soon as he recognized my voice, he said, "I couldn't stand not having more pieces of the puzzle, Mike. I went back to when they were feeding information into the computers and zeroed in on Fells and Bern. We ran constant checks on our men without their knowledge, especially those whose performance was getting shoddy."

"Bern and Fells are dead," I interrupted.

"Killed at the safe house, I presume?"

"Good guess, General."

"It wasn't a guess. That safe house was supposed to be known and used by Bern and Fells only. I have two reports that a third party had access to it on several occasions. No description."

"Penta," I said.

"What makes you think so?"

"You said he was here on a high-level assignment."

"That was a generality."

"Now it's a specific. He had a target ... the vice president. He didn't make it a priority and was probably considered unreliable. Bern and Fells were sent to kill him. The only real contact they had with him was through me, so they tried the interrogation under narcotics in Smiley's garage. Hell, they probably used Smiley's premises before when they were on your team."

"Shall I check on that point?"

"No use, General. One of them came back and knocked off Smiley so nobody would make the connection. Their mistake was using their old safe house again. If they had let slip to Penta when they worked together where that safe house was, he could have used it himself. It wouldn't have been much of a trick to get keys to the place. A nice piece of information to have just in case."

"He used it well," Skubal said. "I imagine he staked it out and killed them both together."

"Looked like a small-caliber hollow-point at close range, right in the heads."

"Penta has used that technique before. One shot each?"

"He didn't need any more."

"What else can keep him in the area, Mike?"

"Explain."

"He killed his first person in your office. He's killed two men assigned to wipe him out. If the reports are correct, nothing is going to keep this Penta from fulfilling his contract."

"Why should somebody want to kill the vice president?"

"No one can really understand the political mind. What happens at those levels aren't mine to consider, outside investigative situations. I collect facts now. However, there is one thing for you to reflect on."

Here it came again and I beat him to it. "He doesn't want me, General."

"If you say so. But somebody wants you. Why?"

I said, "They still think I know where their billion dollars went to."

The word *billion* stopped him momentarily. "For that much money," he told me, "I think they would go to far sterner methods to get you out of the way. Where are you now?"

"In Pat's office. I couldn't be safer."

"You realize, of course, that you're vulnerable. Have you seen the tabloid that's on the newsstand?"

"I picked it up on the way home."

"Then anyone who knows of your true connection with Velda can have a secondary target. Have you checked on her yet?"

"No, I was planning to, but—"

"Get in gear, Michael. That girl had better be kept under close cover. The vice president is under security, money can always wait, but don't let that girl get killed. She was your primary reason for getting involved in this to start with, so keep it that way."

"Okay, General, you got it." He hung up with a grunt before I could say good-bye.

Pat was looking at me, washing a couple of aspirins down with a drink of water. He squashed the cup in his fingers and tossed it in a wastebasket. The clock on the wall said it was five minutes after midnight. He said, "It's tomorrow, pal. I think we should talk."

"You feel it too?"

He nodded. "It's all closing in and I'm sitting on my thumbs. It started out as the murder of a nobody and now we're into all kinds of shit. Over in the other corner you're playing footsies with the Ice Lady and leaving me out in the cold. So let's put the pieces together. Sooner or later they are going to be asking me questions about your involvement and how and why I tolerated it and I'd like it all to go down clean and neat so that I'm off the hook and back on pension drive again. Now, let's do it."

Talk. I pushed myself out of the chair and walked to the window. A few drops of rain hit it and inched down the pane, gradually soaking into the New York grime. Talk. Nothing but air and sounds unless it made sense. I turned around and stared at Pat. He had settled down in the desk chair, slowly folding his hands behind his head. He propped his foot on the toolbox and pushed himself back into a leaning position, waiting for me to talk.

When he saw me grin with my teeth tight and my lips pulled back, he started to frown because he knew something had happened. I picked up the phone. I called Candace again and told her to get down here right away. She got all pissed off this time and insisted I tell her why. I said because she wanted to be president, that's why, and she didn't give me any more argument. I went to the coffee maker, poured a stale cup, stirred in enough sweetener so it didn't matter and sat down on the edge of the desk.

Pat was giving me all the time in the world. I picked up a copy of *Combat Handguns* magazine, October 1988, and read the article titled "The Assassin: Who, When, Where, Why." "Got a later issue?" I asked him.

He shook his head.

I had just started reading the advertisements when Candace came in. She was mad, curious and beautiful, and now Pat took his hands down, leaned forward, waiting to see what I had to say.

"You were on the right track, Pat."

"What?"

"How come you didn't send that toolbox to the property clerk?"

"It's active evidence, that's why." He reached down, picked up the box and set it on the desk.

"Figure it out?"

I got that odd look again. "It didn't belong there. It was a keepsake. His old man made it." He fondled the handle of one of the chisels and put it back again. "You know what's queer here, don't you?"

"Sure," I said. "He had no memory of his past except for the toolbox. They delivered him to his mother's house. He didn't know her, but spotted the box and just took it. He never even said why, except for one word. Mrs. DiCica said he told her 'Papa' and that was all."

"Mike, please," Candace interrupted, "get to the point."

"After he had his brains scrambled, he went to the hospital. His mother picked up his belongings and took them to her house. This toolbox was in his apartment. When he saw it again after his confinement, something registered in his mind.

Something had left an impression heavy enough not to have been wiped out."

I dumped the tools out on Pat's desk, looked at each piece carefully, then put them aside. Nothing was wrong with them at all. So it had to be in the box itself. The construction was sturdy, of hand-fitted three-quarter-inch-thick pine boards, the wood delicately carved and polished. The inch-thick dowel rod that ran the length of the box was worn smooth from constant handling in the center, with clever swirls growing deeper toward the ends. The box itself was more than a repository for tools. It was a personal thing whose maker was artisan as well as carpenter.

And the damn thing was all solid wood. No hidden compartments, no secret places that I could see at all.

But you aren't *supposed* to see secret places. They were made to remain unseen.

I turned the box over and studied the initialed v.d., felt the grooving with my fingertip and probed where it fitted into the sides. Nothing. There wasn't one damn thing out of order.

Pat was getting an exasperated look. There was disgust in his eyes and he pulled his hand across his mouth in an annoyed gesture.

Candace still had some hope. Her eyes never left the box and when I put it back on the desk, finished with the examination, she still couldn't take her eyes off it. She had taken me at my word and saw the presidency sitting there because I had told her I would do it.

Pat said, "I hope this isn't a game, buddy."

I looked down into the empty box trying to think of something to say when I saw something that wasn't there at all. The wood grain of the bottom was typically pine, clear unknotted pine. I turned the box over again and looked at that part, beautifully clear unknotted pine.

But the grain patterns were not identical. Close, but not identical.

There was a famous knot in a rope that nobody could untie until the rough boy took his sword and slashed right through it and that ended that deal.

I picked up the hammer, turned the box over and smashed it into the bottom. I didn't bother to look at how delicately or how cleverly the panel was built into the box . . . I just pulled out the envelope, and three oversize one-hundred-dollar bills from the turn of the century, still redeemable in gold. I handed the bills to Pat and the envelope to Candace.

Pat's face had no expression to it at all. We looked at Candace as she opened the envelope and took out two typed sheets of paper. She glanced at it quickly, her eyes widening abruptly. Then she turned the pages around for us to see.

"It's in code. The whole thing's in code."

I said, "Pat . . . ?"

There was no hesitation. "Let's get Ray Wilson. He can set up the computers and have a go at it."

"Decoding isn't that easy," Candace said.

"Ray can get a few hours in on it before we even get it to the experts in Washington. Send them a copy anyway, but Ray gets first crack at it." He reached for the phone and started to run down Wilson.

"Mike . . ."

"Yeah?"

"You think this is it?"

"What else can it be?"

"If we can locate this cache . . ."

"Don't go getting your hopes up, baby. All you'll get will be the coke. There won't be any line to the buyers or the sellers by now. What you're getting is like digging up a live blockbuster bomb left over from World War II. All it's good for is destruction. You take the potential destructive value away, then everything goes back to square one. The status stays quo. There's no use for the previous owners waiting for the stuff to show up or go on searching for it. It's over."

"But we haven't found it yet," she said.

I could feel my stomach tighten up and I said, "Damn it to hell!"

Pat waved me to stop, but I ignored him and got out of there as fast as I could.

11

Now the rain was making itself felt. It wasn't a clean rain you could shake loose, but a clinging wetness that smelled of concrete and asphalt. This kind of rain hid things you wanted to know and touched all your nerves with an irritating kind of anxiety.

A Yellow Cab with a lady driver pulled over and I got in, giving her the hospital address. Her eyes bounced up to the rearview mirror. "You want emergency?"

"Right."

"You got it, mister." She hauled out into traffic and got heavy on the gas pedal. She made the first light, got right in the sequence and traveled with the green all the way to the turn. She went through a red signal, cut off a truck and went up the ramp as neatly as any ambulance. I handed her a ten-spot and didn't ask for change.

Sickness and injury never stop in the big city. It was a real bloody night in the emergency room, spatters of red on the walls, trails stringing along the floors, smeared where feet had skidded in its sticky viscosity. The walking wounded were crowded by stretchers and wheelchairs and my shortcut to Velda's floor was blocked.

Rather than try to bust on through I ran down the corridor and followed the arrows to the front elevators. I passed a dozen people, doctors and nurses, but running was common in a hospital and nobody questioned me. It was long after visitors' hours and if you were there at this time, you were authorized to be there.

There were three elevators in the bank and all of them were on the upper floors. I wasn't about to wait, found the stairwell and went up them two at a time. I stopped on the third-floor landing, my breath raw in my lungs. I made myself breathe easily and in thirty seconds a degree of normalcy came back. Wasting myself in a wild run up the stairs wouldn't leave anything left, and that I couldn't take a chance on.

When I reached her floor I pushed through the steel fire door into the corridor and the wave of quiet was a soft kiss of relief. The nurse's desk was to my left, the white tip of the attendant's hat bobbing behind the counter. Someplace a phone rang and was answered. Halfway down the hall a uniformed officer was standing beside a chair, his back against the wall, reading a paper.

The nurse didn't look up, so I went by her. Two of the rooms I passed had their doors open and in the half-lit room I could see forms of the patients, deep in sleep. The next two doors were closed and so was Velda's.

Until I was ten feet away the cop didn't give me a tumble, then he turned and scowled at me. This was a new one on the night shift and he pulled back his sleeve and gave a deliberate look at his wristwatch as if to remind me of the time.

There was no sense making waves when there was no water. I said, "Everything okay?"

For a second the question seemed to confuse him. Then he nodded. "Sure," he replied. "Of course."

All I could do was nod back, like it was stupid of me to ask, and I let him go back to leaning against the wall, his feet crossed comfortably. At the desk I edged around the side until the nurse glanced up. She recognized me and smiled. "Mr. Hammer, good evening."

"How's my doll doing?"

"Just fine, Mr. Hammer. Dr. Reedey was in twice today. Her bandages have been changed and one of the nurses has even helped her with cosmetics."

"Is she moving around?"

"Oh, no. The doctor wants her to have complete bed rest for now. It will be several days before she'll be active at all." She stopped, suddenly realizing the time herself. "Aren't you here a little late?"

"I hope not." Something was bothering me. Something was grating at me and I didn't know what it was. "Nothing out of order on the floor?"

She seemed surprised. "No, everything is quite calm, fortunately."

A small timer on her desk pinged and she looked at her watch. "I'll be back in a few minutes, Mr. Hammer . . ."

Now I knew what the matter was. That cop had looked at his watch too and his was a Rolex Oyster, a big fat expensive watch street cops don't wear on duty. But the real kicker was his shoes. They were regulation black, but they were wing tips. The son of a bitch was a phony, but his rod would be for real and whatever was going down would be just as real.

I said, "How long has that cop been on her door?"

"Oh . . . he came in about fifteen minutes ago."

It was two hours too soon for a shift change.

"Did you see the other one check out?"

"Well, no, but he could have gone . . ."

"They always take these elevators down, don't they?"

She nodded, consternation showing in her eyes. She got the picture all at once and asked calmly, "What shall I do?"

"This a scheduled call you make?"

"I have a patient who needs his medication."

"Where are the other nurses?"

"Madge is on her coffee break. I hold down the fort while she goes."

"All right, you go take care of the patient and stay there. What room is he in?"

"The last one down on the right."

"I'll call when I want you. Give me the phone and you beat it. Don't look back. Do things the way you always do."

She patted her hair in place, went around the counter and stepped on down the hall. She didn't look back. I pulled her call sheet over where I could see it and dialed hospital security. The phone rang eight times and nobody answered. I dialed the operator and she tried. Finally she said, "I'll put their code on, sir. The guards must be making their rounds."

Or they're laid out on their backs someplace.

Overhead, the call bell started to ping out a quiet code every few seconds.

I hung up and dialed Pat's office. He wasn't in either. I remembered his trying to get Ray Wilson and had the operator put me through to Ray's office. This time I got him.

I said, "Pat, I have no time for talk. I'm at the hospital and everything's breaking loose. There's a phony cop at the door, so the real officer is down somewhere. They're going to try to snatch Velda. If they wanted her dead, they would have already done it. Get some cars up here and no sirens. They smell cops and they can kill her."

"They moving now?" Pat got in.

I heard wheels rolling on tile and squinted around the wall. Coming out of the last door down on the right was an empty gurney pushed by a man in orderly's clothes. "They're moving. Shake your ass."

I hung up and stepped out into the corridor, whistling between my teeth. The guy pushing the gurney stopped and started playing with the mattress. I pushed the button on the elevator, looked down at the cop who was watching me too and waved. The phony cop waved back.

When the elevator halted, I got in, let the doors close and pushed the STOP button. I stood there, hoping the guy pushing the gurney wouldn't notice the lights over the doors standing still. The rubber tires thumped a little louder, passed the elevator, and when I didn't hear them any longer, I pushed the MANUAL OPEN button and stood there staring out into the empty corridor. I took my hat off, dropped it on the floor and yanked the .45 out of the holster. There was a shell in the chamber and the hammer was on half cock. I thumbed it back all the way and looked down the corridor.

The guy in the orderly's clothes was standing there with an AK47 automatic rifle cradled in his arms watching both ends of the hallway. His stance was low and when he swung, his coat flopped open and it looked like he was wearing upper-body armor. Half the gurney was sticking out Velda's door and even as I watched, it moved out and I saw her strapped onto the carrier. The man in uniform came out with a police service .38 in one hand and one hell of a big bruiser of an automatic in the other. Unless I got some backup, I was totally outgunned and no way I could close in on them without putting Velda's life on the line.

A quiet little code still pinged from the hall bell. Security still hadn't answered.

No wasted moves this time. The pair moved the gurney away from me and I knew they were headed toward the emergency-room exit. The orderly had draped a sheet over the gun on his arm, and the uniform had the .38 on the gurney next to Velda and the automatic hidden someplace in front of him.

I stepped back in the car, let the doors close, pushed the first-floor button and hoped nobody tried to get on. Like all hospital elevators, this one took forever to pass each level and before it stopped, I picked my hat up and held it over my .45. I stepped out. This time I didn't run. The gurney would be moving at proper walking speed, seemingly going through a normal routine, and as long as I hurried, I could meet it outside the building. There was no way this play could be stopped without some kind of shooting, and I didn't want anybody else in the way.

Ahead I could see the entrance to the emergency room and the elevator bank they would come out of. Now they had two options, going through the crowd, taking the risk of having their weapons spotted, or heading for the walkway door where I was standing. It wasn't made for gurneys, but it was ramped for wheelchairs and with some juggling, a gurney could get through.

They came out of the elevator just as I stepped outside and now I felt better. They had turned toward the walkway door and I was waiting out there in the dark. There were only a few seconds to look around for their probable course and find cover. The walkway curved down to the street, but the parking places were filled again with off-street overnighters, and the cars there couldn't handle a limp patient. Unless they had planned on a mobile van or station wagon, any transportation would have to be farther down the line, out of sight from where I was standing.

I moved on down the walk, reached the parked cars and got in the street behind them. The doors of the building swung inward. The guy in the orderly uniform came out first, the AK47 under his arm, still covered by a cloth of some kind. He never took his eyes off the area in front of him, juggling the gurney forward with one hand while the other man pushed from behind. It finally slid through and now the phony cop had the over-sized automatic in his hand, the holstered .38 ready to grab.

Risking a shot was crazy. The pair were alert,

well armed and probably handy with their equipment. They most likely had preplanned an escape exit if they were intercepted, and killing Velda would be a part of the play. I'd have to get off two perfect shots on the first try with a six-foot spread between targets in dim light at a bad distance, and I wasn't that good to try.

The gurney made the sidewalk and the two cranked it into a turn going away from the hospital. Both of them were still facing forward, both right on the edge of action. I let them pass me, crouching down behind the bodies of the cars, and when they were about ten feet in front, I kept pace with their movements.

A car turned up the road, momentarily lighting up the area. The beam swept over the gurney, but the two went on in a normal manner. I stepped between the parked cars and let the car pass. It was an unmarked sedan with a woman at the wheel. It seemed like an hour had passed, but it had only been a few minutes.

Hell, traffic was light. A squad car could have been here by now. Another set of lights turned up, a truck dropped down a gear and lumbered up the hill. I moved down two car lengths, still staying close, still silently swearing at the frustrating delays in emergency police actions. A car made the U-turn at the hospital and came toward me from the other direction and only when it got past me did a raucous blast from a loudhailer yell, "Freeze! Police!" and the power lights from the truck turned night into day, blinding the two men in the glare.

Everything happened so quickly there was a hesitancy in the movements the men made. The orderly wasted one second trying to strip the cloth from the AK47 and a pair of rapid blasts took him down and out. The phony cop jammed himself down in a crouch and his gun came up to shoot through the bottom of the gurney. He was out of sight of the others, but not out of mine, and I squeezed off a single round that took him in the shoulder and spun him around like a rag doll.

I was standing and had my hands over my head so the cops wouldn't take me out with a wild shot figuring me for the other side. Pat came running up, a snub-nosed .38 in his fist, and said, "You okay, Mike?"

"No sweat." I took my hands down in time to yell and half-point behind Pat, and he turned and fired at the phony cop who had pulled his .38 out of the holster and was about to let go at the gurney again. Pat put one into the side of his head, blowing his brains all over the sidewalk.

They all came out one side, so his face was gory, but still recognizable.

The area was cordoned off so fast no spectators had a chance to get near the bodies. Two cops took the gurney out to the truck, lifted it in the back way, and the lady cop from the first car got in with Velda and the unit lurched ahead, made a turn in the street and headed west.

Pat took my arm and hustled me toward his own unmarked cruiser close by. I said, "Where did you guys come from?"

"Come on, pal, I alerted this team as soon as you headed over here." He yanked a portable radio from his pocket and said into it, "Charlie squad, what have you got?"

There was a click and a hum and a flat voice answered with, "One officer down in the patient's room, Captain. We have a doctor here who says he was sapped, then drugged. There are two syringes on the bed table, both empty."

"Is the officer okay?"

"Vital signs okay, the doc says."

I tapped Pat on the shoulder. "Tell him to check the last room down the hall on the right."

He passed the message on and a minute later the receiver hummed and the voice said, "Got a nurse down in there too, Captain. She got the same treatment. The patient who was here is gone."

"He sure is," Pat told him.

We went to get into the car when the radio came alive again. Pat barked a "Go ahead" and the cop on the other end said, "Captain, four hospital security guys just got here. They answered a call in the basement and wound up locked in a storeroom."

"Good. Get a statement from them and check both those rooms out."

"Roger, Captain."

He turned the key and put the car in gear. Up ahead the truck was turning the corner and he leaned on the gas to catch up to it. "Mind telling me where we're going?"

"For tonight you're going fancy. The Ice Lady is putting you two up in her apartment."

"Great," I said.

"What's that supposed to mean?"

"Nothing."

"You two aren't going to be targets any more. The crap's over, finished. Dr. Reedey is meeting us at Candace's to check Velda out. We'll hold you there overnight and get you squared away tomorrow. If you two weren't friends, I'd slap both of you in a prison ward to keep you out of trouble."

"Did you get a good look at the guy you shot?"

"I got a good look at both of them."

"Make 'em?"

He yanked on the wheel, pulling around a car and coming up directly behind the truck. "The slob playing cop was Nolo Abberniche. He started out as a kid with the Costello bunch. That bastard has knocked off a half dozen guys and all he has are three arrests on petty offenses."

"You seem to have a good line on him."

"Plenty of fliers, nationwide inquiries. Pal, you are traveling in some pretty heavy company. That other guy was Marty Santino. He's another hit man, but he likes the fancy jobs. This one was right up his alley."

"Who's paying for it, Pat?"

"That died with those hoods. You know damn well we won't find anything to tie them in directly with any of the mob boys, but we sure as hell know there's a connection somewhere."

"Beautiful," I said. "We wait for them to make another run on us."

"Not this time, Mike. You drop the code leading to a truckload of coke down our throats and we're going to treat you like royalty until it shows up. They don't know we own Anthony DiCica's little secret. Well, once it's in our hands they can go back to business as usual. You're going to be our little secret too."

"What's that supposed to mean?" I asked him.

"Simple, pal. We're taking you and Velda right out of the action. Both of you are too important as witnesses and possible targets to be exposed during the mop-up. I know damn well you're not going to let her out of your sight, so we're setting both of you up at a safe house of our choosing. Any objections?"

"No."

"Good. I thought you'd do it my way for once. You'll be covering Velda and we'll be covering both of you just in case. It may seem redundant, but we don't want to take any chances."

I nodded and looked back at the buildings passing by.

The truck slowed, edging toward the curb, and pulled to a stop in front of the apartment building. The way the doorman came out to run us off you'd think we were from Mars, but when the blue uniforms showed, he backed off fast, held the doors open while the gurney came out and helped get it on the service elevator. I squeezed on beside it, and when I did, Velda's eyes fluttered, then opened, and she looked at me. She didn't know what had happened or where she was, but she knew me and smiled.

Candace was waiting at her apartment and she wasn't alone. Bennett Bradley and Lewis Ferguson were deep in conversation, and Coleman and Carmody were at the bar. They stopped what they were doing to help get Velda into the bedroom where Burke Reedey was laying out his supplies. There was nothing I could do so I went to the bar and made a drink for myself.

"Make one for me too, please," Candace said.

I mixed the highball, turned around and handed it to her. "Appreciate your lending us the apartment."

"And I appreciate your trying to make me president."

"They shoot at presidents," I said.

"They shoot at cops too."

We clinked glasses, each taking a good pull at a drink. "How is Ray doing with the code?"

"All we can do is wait. He's linked in with Washington and Langley, and all we know is that it isn't an ultrasophisticated concept. Apparently he had a working knowledge of codes, and with the repetition the computers can deliver, it shouldn't take long."

"Who's going on the bust?"

"A select group. We're assuming it's within driving distance and the coordination is coming under federal jurisdiction. They can organize assistance from any local police departments if they have to."

"Where do you stand?"

"In the catbird seat, my wonderful friend." She looked past me and pointed.

Pat was finishing with the cops who had brought Velda up and was waving me over to the table where the men were conferring over a map. They had circled out an area in New York State northwest of Kingston with Phoenicia as a hub. Ferguson was a ski buff and knew the area well, but best of all, he had access to a cottage in the mountainous section and had outlined the entry roads and was explaining the place's benefits.

"From the building there is good three-hundred-sixty-degree visibility. Power comes in from the road, but the place is equipped with emergency Coleman lanterns, a hand pump for water if the power goes out, and always has a good supply of split logs on hand for the fireplace."

He shaded in a section on the map and explained, "The house sits ... here." He tapped the pencil to indicate the spot. "And approximately fifty yards away toward the road are two stone outcroppings, excellent positions as guard posts. A man can be stationed at both positions with a good field of fire that would cover anyone trying to gain entry."

"What about the rear?" I asked him.

"A sheer cliff almost sixty feet high. They'd have to drop in by parachute. The foliage is just too thick for anybody to break through up there without a dozen machetes or brushhooks."

Pat said, "We're not dealing with trained woodsmen, Mike."

"You can buy them, kiddo."

"Not as fast as we can move."

I took another jolt of the highball. "Let's give the other side a little credit. Suppose they had an observer at the hospital to catch the action. Suppose he saw what was going on and followed the truck back here."

"What's your point, Mike?"

"How are we getting out of this place without being spotted? They have men, money and machinery going for them too. They could have spotters with radios as well as the cops."

Pat gave me one of his noncommittal gestures again. "Suppose you just let us take care of that."

After what he pulled with the blast at the hospital, I had to give him the benefit of the doubt. "Sure, pal, sorry," I said. I finished the drink and went back for another one. Candace had it ready for me. For the first time that evening I took a close look at her. There was no dress this time, just a beautifully tailored khaki jumpsuit that would look fashionable as hell at a cocktail party or would be casually efficient for a field sweep. Whatever she had in mind, she was ready for it. Those big sensual eyes were almost iridescent with anticipation, and the tautness of her body showed right through the twill of the jumpsuit.

She knew I was going to say something.

She was waiting to hear it.

The phone rang. Instantly, the room went quiet. She picked up the receiver. When she scanned the room with one quick glance and nodded, we knew she was talking to Ray Wilson. She picked up a ballpoint pen, stripped a page off the pad beside the phone and began writing down the instructions. She finished, thanked him and hung up.

"We have the location of the truck," she said. "It's in a barn on a farm north of Lake Hopatcong on Route Ninety-four, just before coming into Hamburg."

Bennett Bradley said, "I'll alert the Jersey highway patrol, and they can pick us up on the other side of the George Washington Bridge with an escort."

"You want any county police on this?"

"Forget it," Bradley told him. "We don't want

to divulge any details of the site." He went back to the map they were using for our relocation and found what he was looking for. "Here," he said. "We'll have two more cars meet us at the junction of Routes Fifteen and Ninety-four." He picked up the phone, called the operator for the number of the Jersey highway patrol, then dialed it.

Ferguson was thumbing through a pocket-size pad of his own and told Carmody, "If we start crossing agency lines on this, we'll have one hell of a mess. Now, who wants it?"

"How many men do you think we'll need?" Carmody asked him.

"At least a dozen, heavily armed, to guard that stuff. We may be able to keep the raid quiet, but we can't plan on it."

"That load has got to be moved out. If the trailer's in good shape, we'll need a tractor to haul it and at least four mobile units for cover. The state guys can lead and be the tail on the convoy."

"Okay," Frank Carmody told him. "This whole thing is going to be interstate, so let me handle it. The FBI can get on this from our local offices a lot faster than Langley can. That satisfactory?"

"Fine by me," Ferguson agreed. "I'll stay on this end getting Hammer and his lady out of the area. Now, what's the time schedule going to be like?"

Both of them glanced at Bradley, who was

putting the phone down. "That guy's ready right now," Carmody muttered.

"He wants to make some points before his replacement gets here. Can't blame him at all. However, he waits on this one. That stuff has been there so long a few more days won't matter. The major thing is *we* know where it is and we don't want to chance losing it at this point by a lot of hasty maneuvering."

Bradley came back, smiling gently, then raised his eyebrows at Carmody and Ferguson. "You two would make terrible poker players."

Carmody frowned, annoyed. "What?"

"I don't plan to barge right in on this," Bradley told him.

You could see the relief on their faces.

Bradley said, "One car will make the run first. We want the exact location, photos taken of the area, then we'll regroup for a final planning. The Jersey police will be given full authorization to work this under our command and will move on it the minute we call them."

"Who's going in the car?"

"Guess," Candace said.

"You think that's practical?" Ferguson asked her.

"A man and a woman riding together is a natural, gentlemen. Besides, I'm the only one who knows the fine details of the terminal point. Mr. Bradley and I will make a good team."

Bradley gave her a smile and a half bow. "It's settled then."

"And when do Velda and I move out?" I asked.

It was Ferguson who said, "First thing in the morning, buddy. We want to get you out of here at first light and settled in with guards on post before nightfall."

"Velda's going to need clothes."

Candace said, "We're both about the same size. I can outfit her with what she'll need."

I was going to object, but Pat stopped me. "Do it that way, Mike. And you can pick up what you need from any store in the area. I wouldn't suggest your going back to your apartment. You got any cash on you?"

"Enough," I told him.

"How much ammo you got for your forty-five?"

"Two full clips."

"Pick up a box."

"Who am I supposed to kill, Pat?"

For the second that he said nothing, I saw the note in my mind. *You die for killing me.*

"I'm sure you'll find somebody," Pat said jokingly.

Burke Reedey had changed Velda's bandage and helped her straighten up her hair. Under the makeup the signs of discoloration had almost faded and the swelling around her eye was nearly gone. Her lips were back to their natural shape and fullness, and I sat on the edge of the gurney and laid my palm against her cheek. "How you doing, baby?"

Her smile started before her eyes opened, then she said, "At least I'm not pregnant."

"Clever thought."

"Life around you is never dull, Mike. Dangerous, but never dull."

"Sorry, kitten." My fingers brushed the edges of her hair lightly.

"Burke didn't want to tell me what happened."

"How much do you remember?"

She closed her eyes, thought about it a moment and looked up at me. "I had been asleep. The doctor had given me a sedative. There seemed to be some noise that wakened me, and I knew somebody was in the room, but I thought it was Burke who had come back. Then a needle went into my arm and I was back asleep again. There were shots. I do remember shots, but they were part of my sleep." Her eyes narrowed discernibly. "They *were* shots, weren't they?"

"Two guys who tried to snatch you were killed."

"You?"

"I hit one in the arm, but Pat knocked him off. Snipers got the other one."

"Mike . . . why me?"

"To hurt me, doll. They still thought they could squeeze me for information I didn't even have, if they had you."

"What's happened?"

"Now we know what they want. That's why we're getting off the scene until this event is over."

"Since when do *you* cut out, Mike?" Her voice had an angry tone.

"When you need somebody to cover your ass, doll. Now shut up and take it as it comes." I leaned forward, cradling her head in my hands, and kissed her mouth. Then her hands came up and held me too, and our mouths were soft and gentle together, full of warmth that I had missed so badly.

Behind me, Candace coughed softly, and I eased Velda back. Burke had given her another sedative and she was getting sleepy. She had another jumpsuit outfit over her arm. "Let me dress her now," she said. "Then she'll be ready for the trip."

I nodded and went outside, half closing the door. Pat was on the telephone, two new plainclothes cops were in the room, and the other three were bent over the map again.

Five minutes later Candace came out and shut the door gently. "There's a suitcase of casual things and some underwear by the door. My shoes will be a little oversize on her, but it won't matter."

"Thanks, I appreciate it."

"I saw the way you kissed her."

"We're old friends."

"Bullshit. Why don't you just say you love her?"

"Why do girls always think—"

"Because we're jealous, Mike. When a girl's

not in love, she's jealous of anybody else who is."

"You know . . ."

Candace put her finger on my mouth. "Don't say anything silly, big boy. We had a few wild moments and it was good. Crazy, but very good. You realize it never would have lasted for us."

I grinned at her and gave her hip a little pat. "Call me when the screwballs think they have you cornered."

"When will that be?"

"When you're president, kiddo."

Pat turned that sharp look on me when I said the word, and we both remembered we still had Penta in the picture somewhere. He was going to eliminate the vice president of the United States, but first he had to finish a job for himself.

12

The trip upstate started before dawn. It began with a ride in a police cruiser to the local precinct station, a switch to an unmarked car with us stretched out on the floor in the rear, winding up at the Fourth Precinct downtown with a shuffle to another car, indistinguishable in the shuffle of vehicles coming and going in the vicinity.

Now Ferguson was driving and I rode in the backseat with Velda's head on my shoulder, while two other cars hung back a few hundred feet, the occupants from the bureau's local office. Ferguson knew them all and assured me they were good men.

We crossed the bridge, headed north and picked

up the New York State Thruway at Suffern and stayed at speed limit while the guard cars played little games to make sure nobody was following us. At our speed nearly everybody passed and kept on going or turned off at the exit ramps.

All the cars had constant radio communication and when we got to Kingston, we all turned off the thruway and gassed up. I found a store to pick up the clothes I needed, got a flashlight, extra batteries and a box of .45s. When we loaded up again, we picked up Route 28 going northwest and practically had the road to ourselves.

Now it was Ferguson's backyard. He knew where he was headed, took us past Mt. Tremper, through Phoenicia, and a few miles farther on he radioed the other cars he was turning off, would continue for a half mile and stop while they did the same thing a quarter mile up. If anybody was doing a delayed-action tailing job, they'd be spotted coming off the main road.

Where he pulled up was a shale-topped drive that had earmarks of having been long in use, but not very often. When we stopped, we waited for a full fifteen minutes before the all clear was given, then we drove ahead at slow speed, took a righthand fork for another half mile, then broke out of the woods that had surrounded us onto a grassy plain, and there ahead was the house and the rock outcroppings that made natural guardposts.

Velda had slept through most of the trip. Now

the sedative had worn off and she was having a rebirth, being in new surroundings, knowing her body was knitting together properly. Ferguson got our luggage and opened the cabin up while I got Velda out of the car and onto her feet. She was shaky and held on to my arm, taking each step carefully.

"Going to make it or do I carry you?"

"Across the threshold?"

I gave her a squeeze. "I think you're strong enough to walk this one."

Her elbow nudged my ribs. "A girl can always hope." Her grin had a pixie twist to it and I knew she was better. She was my girl again, the beautiful doll with the deep auburn page-boy hair that had a piece cut out of it now. The svelte-bodied beauty who still had colorful blue and purple shadows around one eye. The lush-hipped, full-breasted delight of a woman whom I had almost lost.

"What are you thinking, Mike?"

"No way I'm going to tell you that," I said, and gave her a little laugh. I didn't have to tell her anyway. She already knew. I moved her to a big, soft La-Z-Boy chair, got her comfortable and went to help Ferguson and the others get the place ready.

Two of the agency men who never seemed to have anything to say got their gear together, large thermos bottles of coffee, water canteens, packages of food, and rolled everything up in their watertight ponchos. Each one carried a holstered sidearm and a Colt AR-15A2 rifle chambered for a .223 cartridge, a fast-firing, accurate rifle with deadly capabilities. Each one was equipped with a night scope. A metal case held the spare clips. When they were satisfied, they strode off to the rock outcroppings. Neither one had said anything at all.

Ferguson came in from the kitchen and handed me a set of keys. "I'm leaving my car around the back in case you need it. It's out of sight, got plenty of gas and is facing forward in case you have to make a quick getaway."

"Why would I do that?"

"Just a precaution." He took a compact walkie-talkie from his pocket, thumbed the button and said, "Number one, check."

The radio said, "One, check."

"Number two, check."

"Two, check," the radio repeated.

He thumbed the switch off and laid the walkie-talkie on the table. "You have emergency contact with both guard positions. And for Pete's sake, keep radio silence as much as possible. Let them alert you if possible. When their radios are receiving, other ears as well as theirs can hear them."

"Got it," I said. "The phone working here?"

"Yeah, but the damn thing's on a party line, so stay off it."

"How about television?"

"You lucked in. They ran cable in here last year, so amuse yourself on thirty channels. Everything else is in working order, you got groceries, beer and plenty of toilet paper. You want any smokes?"

"I quit."

"Then enjoy yourself, pardnuh. Be nice to the lady."

"Do me a favor, Ferguson."

"Like what?"

"Have Pat call me when the bust goes down."

Ferguson held out his hand and I took it. He said, "Sure thing, Mike," then went outside with the others. The engines of two cars came to life, then slowly faded out of earshot down the road.

The sun had gone down behind the mountain and the shadow threw an early veil of darkness around the house. I made the rounds, locking the windows and doors, familiarizing myself with the place. The living room was a good size, the fireplace functional as well as ornamental. Both bedrooms were done in rugged Early American style, a bathroom opening off each one. The kitchen was a cook's dream and whoever spent time here was in the country without losing any of the benefits of modern civilization.

I checked out the porches, all the closets, and in the hallway I spotted an almost hidden ceiling hatch. I pulled a chair over, stepped up onto it, pushed the hatch cover up and stuck my head into the opening, probing the darkness with my flashlight.

Batts of insulation ran between the floor beams and most of the area was covered with sheets of plywood to provide storage space, but now there was nothing there but the roof supports and the hand-laid brickwork of the massive fireplace chimney. I pulled the hatch cover back in place and got down off the chair.

The windows had curtains that were nearly opaque and I closed them before I snapped on the TV set and let it give us all the light we needed. I brought over two egg salad sandwiches, opened the coffee thermos, poured out two cups and sat down beside Velda.

She said, "Tell me about it. From the beginning. Don't leave anything out."

So I told her from the beginning, but I did leave some things out. She asked questions and had me repeat events several times, putting the pieces of the picture in a framework that would contain something recognizable. Inside there she was looking for Penta too, searching for the killer who had almost killed her. There was no anger in the way she was thinking, simply a purposeful, quiet deliberateness that poked and prodded at the pieces, trying to get them to fit. I talked to her, held hands while she pondered, and when she came to the same blank stone wall that somebody had scrawled the name Penta on, she said, "I'm tired, Mike."

I got her into the bedroom and she turned around, put her arms around my neck and said in a tired voice, "Do me."

My fingers unzipped the jumpsuit, let it fall, then unsnapped her bra. She shrugged out of that too, letting herself sink to the edge of the bed. I pushed her back gently and pulled the covers up round her. "Good night, Tiger," I said.

There was no answer. She was already asleep.

I went back to the living room and sat in a wooden rocker. The news on TV was nothing spectacular. I tried CNN and caught a flurry of national stuff and the day's sports. There was nothing about a billion-dollar drug bust. I pulled a blanket off the other bed, turned off the TV, stretched out in the La-Z-Boy recliner and went to sleep with the .45 in my hand.

The sun came up the east slope, and I threw the window curtains open. The whole area was clear outside, and I picked up the walkie-talkie and said, "Either of you guys want breakfast?"

One said, "You go first, Eddie. I still have some coffee left."

There was no answer, but I saw some movement beside the clump of rocks and the one called Eddie started to trot toward the house, the rifle slung over his shoulder. Everything was real military double time with those two.

I held the door open, let him through and locked it behind him.

"You got hot water? I need a quick shower."

"Try the bathroom. They told me it all works."

I went to the kitchen and started the coffee going. There were eggs, bacon and precooked biscuits in the refrigerator, and I got them all out, cooked them up just as Eddie came out of the bathroom dressed, with damp hair, and still carrying the rifle. He ate, said thanks and went to the door. "I'll send Tunney down," he told me over his shoulder.

Tunney needed a shower too. He ate, had a second cup of coffee and said it had been a quiet night. During the day he and Eddie would each grab some sleep while the other stood guard. At suppertime they would come up one at a time, grab a bite before dark, refill their thermoses and canteens and get set for the night's watch.

The phone rang. I picked it up and Ferguson's voice said, "Everything all right?"

I said, "Great."

He said, "Fine," and hung up.

From Velda's bedroom I heard the sound of a shower running. I went back to the stove again. This morning I had the feeling Velda was going to have her old appetite back. The bacon strips were almost done. I made a square of them in the pan and cracked two eggs into the opening. I basted the eggs the way she liked them and they were done just as she came to the table. I laid out the biscuits and poured us coffee.

"Don't say it," I told her.

"You'll make a great wife, Mike."

"I told you not to say it."

"So punch me in the mouth with your lips," she told me.

"Wait till you swallow your egg," I told her.

We sat through another day and watched a steady stream of television block out hours and half hours. The news had nothing at all. The weather channel said a cold front was moving into our area and we could expect an early frost this year.

At ten minutes to four the phone rang again. Pat said, "The front car was confirmed."

"How soon you going in?"

"On the way, pal."

"Any problems?"

"Only political. B. B. will smooth things out."

I heard a click and a small lessening in the volume of Pat's voice. "Fine," I said, "see you," and hung up. I wanted to say something else to the party on the line, but I didn't bother.

Velda was sitting on the edge of her chair. "It's going down?"

"Bradley and Candace Amory have located the site. Pat said there's a political problem."

"What kind?"

"He didn't say, but it sounds like an inter-agency squabble. Bennett Bradley is going to handle it, and he damn well better be a good diplomat on this one. A hit like this is so big everybody wants a cut of it."

"Damn," she said, "can they mess it up?"

"They can mess up a headhunter's picnic."

"What do we do?"

"Wait . . . and hope they can keep a lid on this."

She looked at me very seriously, her lower lip clenched between her teeth. "This isn't the way it's supposed to be, is it?"

"No."

"There's trouble. You can feel it too, can't you?"

I nodded. It was like that first Saturday when it all started. It was the way the big city so far away was able to swallow its victims and make them disappear without anyone knowing or caring.

The mountain shadow was coming down again.

I fixed coffee and sandwiches for the guys outside, gave them a fast call and Eddie came in, picked up supper for them both and went back to his vigil. Velda and I had a snack and went back to TV, staying on the local New York channel. So far nothing had happened.

At nine o'clock the weather predictions came true. The cold front had come in on schedule and was making itself felt. Velda pulled the blanket up to her neck and shivered.

"Want me to make a fire?"

"That would be nice."

I got the logs together and laid them up on the firedogs, stuffing some loose kindling under them, making a nice neat arrangement. "This is stupid," I said.

"Why?"

"Trying to keep comfortable while a damn killer's playing a game with us."

"It was *his* game, Mike."

"The slob didn't have to leave that note."

"Yes, he did."

"Why? Explain that. Why?"

"Mike . . . how did you kill him?"

I stood up and looked around the mantelpiece. "You see a can of fire starter around?"

"No. You didn't answer me."

"Screw it." I looked on both sides of the fireplace.

"Use the newspapers," she told me.

They were neatly stacked against the wall, about two weeks' worth of *The New York Times*. I grabbed a handful, squatted down and began stripping the pages out, twisting them into cylinders to go under the kindling.

I used up one day's edition and pulled the second one over and nearly ripped the front page off when the thing popped right off the page at me, a two-column photo of a face I hadn't seen in four years and an accompanying article headlined FRANCISCO DUVALLE DIES TONIGHT.

And now, Francisco DuValle was already dead.

"What is it, Mike?"

"They finally executed DuValle," I said.

She took the paper from my hand and read the article. "He had appealed the death sentence for four years. They just came to an end."

"It was my testimony that decided the case. Remember?"

"The verdict was justified. He was a deliberate murderer."

I took the page back and stared at the photo. The face seemed expressionless unless you knew him, because behind the black mask of a heavy, pointed Vandyke beard and an unruly mop of hair that swept forward across his forehead, there was anger and hatred that had erupted into fourteen murders. The eyes appeared flat, but in court they glistened and burned at anybody who had accused him.

When I was on the stand identifying him, they tried to eat me alive. He sat there, tight with controlled anger, not caring that what I said was true, but that his pleasure in the death act had been taken from him. I should have shot him instead of coldcocking him when he made that last attack on the girl, but I hadn't realized who I was taking out.

As I left the stand he said very softly, "You'll die, Hammer. I'll kill you." The guys in the press box heard it and a couple even reported it.

Velda was watching my face as I studied the picture. I could feel myself getting tight as DuValle's soft voice came back to me. My teeth were clenched so tight my jaws ached and she said, "What is it, Mike?"

I turned the page toward her. "Familiar?"

"Only from the court. I was there at the sentencing."

I frowned and said, "Of course . . . how could you see a connection? You only had a short contact and that under stress."

She still didn't get it. "With whom?"

"Have you got any of that makeup they use to cover up your black eye?"

"Erase? It's in my pocketbook."

"Get it."

She brought the tube over and uncapped it. It was a soft white creamy stick, and I laid the paper on the floor and used it on the photo. Carefully, I wiped off the Van Dyke, then took off the mop of hair. Now Duvalle was bald-headed, clean-shaven, and when I trimmed back the ends of the droopy adornment on his upper lip to form a conservative-style mustache, Velda saw the incredible similarity too.

She said, "It's Bennett Bradley."

"No," I told her. "It's Francisco DuValle. They're brothers."

"Mike . . . you'd better be sure."

"I'm sure, doll." I took another long look at the doctored photograph and said, "Penta. I finally got that bastard on the surface."

Francisco DuValle had said it, and Bradley had heard of it, and how he had to do it. *You die for killing me.*

All this time I had played myself for being the innocent bystander when I was the prime target. I had gone off on a wild-assed goose chase, putting Tony DiCica in the middle and getting one hell of a haul of coke and a possible presidential candidate when all the time the slob I wanted who damn near wiped out Velda was standing right there in front of me.

Stupid. I was stupid. And Bradley-Penta loved the chase. It got everybody involved and took all the heat off him. He could operate any way he wanted and all the blame would go in a different direction.

"How could it happen, Mike?"

"Maybe there was a genetic similarity, kitten. Both of them were cold killers. They made a damn study of the subject and killing became part of their lives. They just had different targets, that's all. DuValle went for the pleasure of killing. It was a sensual thing with him. He got off on each murder, enjoying the entire, senseless act. He was hard to run down because there was no motive except pleasure, like so many of the other serial killers.

"But Bradley, he made a profession out of it. Imagine the audacity of a man like that who could promote himself through the ranks to a position in the State Department. Damn!"

Velda couldn't quite comprehend it. She said, "But State would run a check on him, Mike, they don't simply—"

"Kid, his name most likely *is* Bradley. His early background could pass inspection, and no one knew about his current activities. He came in as an expert on Penta. Certainly he knew all about him. He could make his case histories look great, almost coming down on the guy, nearly nailing him and missing so closely they couldn't afford to let him go."

"You said he had a replacement coming in."

"Sure. He even arranged his own transfer as part of his cover. He was given an assignment to assassinate the vice president of the United States by an unfriendly nation because in his position he could work in those circles. He accepted the contract, probably made some deliberate errors on the Penta job that made State recall him, and got reassigned here."

"There was no attempt made on the vice president's life, Mike."

"No, because before he could lay the groundwork, they executed his brother and his mind went into one of those crazy turns that comes with being out of balance. He flipped, really flipped.

"For the first time he acted out of context. He was going to make his brother's promise come true. He knew about me, knew where I lived and where I worked. He had the whole scenario planned out and made arrangements to meet me that Saturday. His loose point was that he didn't know what I looked like. All he had to do was check a newspaper morgue, and he wouldn't have missed. My photo files are an inch thick. All that expertise he had developed went down the drain because he got emotional about a kill."

While I was telling her, I had jammed more paper under the logs. The matches were in a small cast-iron box on the mantel. I lit one and touched the papers off and we watched the fire take hold.

"Funny," I said. "In a way it didn't matter at all. That super ego trip he went on in leaving the Penta note got him right back in the business again. He was the only expert on Penta that State had and he was here, on the spot. *Now* he knew me. *Now* he wouldn't be careless again.

"What Bradley didn't realize was that his bosses overseas had a different way of thinking. They're fanatically nationalistic and had paid him for a political hit and instead he had opened himself up to a possible capture and interrogation which would disclose their scheme, and they wanted him dead."

She picked up the poker and stirred the fire. It was starting to catch, the dry logs beginning to crackle.

"There's no love lost in this crime business. Fells and Bern were old contemporaries of his. He had probably used them on his jobs, so they had a close-knit deal going for them for years. They were bound to know a lot about each other during those years. Now suddenly Bern and Fells get a contract offered them to hit Bradley for not going after his primary target."

"How would they know where to find him?"

"All they knew was what the newspapers mentioned about the note, but that was enough. I was their lead to Penta. They thought I would *have* to know something about him, thus the snatch."

"They could have killed you."

"No. They had too much professional in them. That would bring too much heat down anyway."

"They killed Smiley," she reminded me.

"Honey, those two were real jellybeans. They were in a hurry and used their old contacts on the job. When they got done with Smiley, they didn't want to leave any witness around so they snuffed him. Stupidly, they used an old place that was a safe house once without realizing Penta . . . or Bradley, knew about it too. Even Bradley's timing was great. He was always presumed to be doing something else."

"Scratch Fells and Bern," she mused.

"Two quick, accurate shots and gone. Too bad he didn't have time to shake the place down. Maybe he tried, but that house was set up by experts and those two had a clever hiding place." I let out a laugh. "I wonder if it's still owned by the government."

"Mike . . . when I was in the hospital . . ."

"That first orderly in your room was him. He wanted you dead, kitten."

"That's crazy!"

"Look . . . you *might* have had a quick look at him in our office."

"But I didn't."

"But you *did* have a tape of his voice. Someplace around there would be other tapes he made and a voice-print from yours would be another point of proof that could nail him. One thing. He wasn't dumb. He knew he'd made that call and wanted to double-check on it."

"Making that tape was almost accidental. I never thought . . ."

"He couldn't take the chance. Secondly, he wanted me to make myself vulnerable. He knew damn well I'd go ape if you got knocked off and come right out in the open. Luckily, Pat kept the cops on your door and stymied anything from him in *that* direction. Hell, he was getting plenty of openings on me anyway. He was there when I said I was going to the office and had plenty of time while I was there to get in position and damn near nail me from the car."

I stopped, looked at the fire and thought back to the way I'd kept sloughing off the motive. It was as though there had been none at all.

"You know what the pitiful thing is?" I said. "I was the one who couldn't see it. I got going on the DiCica bit and everything I did was a cover for Bradley. He was on top of the whole deal like the lid on a jar and everything was going his way in spades. If he could assist in nailing that drug cache, there would be no demotion . . . he'd go up another notch and be even more important to his employers than ever. He'd be able to pull off political assassinations almost at will.

"Look how he put himself into the middle of

it. He didn't want any suspicion thrown on him now at all. He volunteers for the scout car with Candace, gives his report to our guys, but someplace he's stopped long enough to alert both federal agencies and get them in a political scuffle. He's supposedly off somewhere smoothing ruffled feathers while the bust is going on, and do you know where he is?"

"Where?" she asked. I could feel the tension in her voice.

"He's on the way back here," I said. "He can make his hit on us and still get back in the play in the city. Nobody will have missed him in all the excitement, or have bothered to look for him, since he would have already planted an alibi."

The fire was blazing away by now, but Velda shivered and I was getting that feeling again. I was computing hours and minutes and knew that what I had just said was true.

I gave Velda a yank away from the brightness of the fire, and we darted in the shadows where the phone was. I picked it up, listened and tapped the bar twice, then put it down.

"The line's cut, isn't it?" Velda asked.

"It would have to be at the main road. There are no poles around here so the wires must go underground out to Route Twenty-eight."

"You can tell the guards—"

"No. He'd have a two-way on this frequency with him. If the guard are on their toes, they might pick him up with those night scopes."

"Might?" There was an odd note of finality in her voice.

Time was going by fast. I had to get in the game and Velda wasn't going to be able to move with me. I said, "Come here," and pulled her into the hallway. I got the chair over, stood up and shoved the hatch cover back. "You're going up there."

She pulled back, her eyes on the black hole in the ceiling. "I can't."

"Nuts. You have to. I had to force her onto the chair, then lift her up into the darkness. When her feet were inside, I handed her the flashlight. At least she had something to hold on to. I told her to stay quiet and don't move, then felt for the hatch and put it back in place.

There was no way I could douse the fire, so I pushed a couple of chairs together in front of the TV, propped enough pillows from the sofa in them to make it look like they were occupied and went to the back bedroom and slid the window open. I crawled out, closed the window and stood there, trying to catch any sound while my eyes adjusted to the night.

When we first got there, I had imprinted the area on my mind and now I was bringing it all back into focus. If Bradley was out there, he could have night-vision glasses on him that could pick up any movement on the terrain.

I went down on my belly, crawling and stopping, trying to bury myself in the grass. Bradley wouldn't have had time for a ground survey like I had, so any small contour I might make could just be a hillock to him. The arc I made took me away from the rock outcropping, circled around it, then I came in from the other end.

Now I could see where the guard was. It was Eddie's station, and I could see him, a vague silhouette against the light. I didn't want him to make any sudden turn and blow me away so I didn't say anything until I was there, right on top of him, and reached out my hand and grabbed his arm.

The damn gun toppled out of his fingers and he fell over on me, the blood wet and sticky from where it was seeping out of his head. I picked up the rifle and sighted it at the other rock hill. What was night became a greenish-tinted dusk where everything was dim, but discernible. I turned the night scope on the other pile of rocks and saw a pair of legs sticking out where they shouldn't be and threw the rifle down.

The bastard was here! Damn it, I should have stayed in the house instead of trying to contact the guard posts. He'd had all the time he needed to nullify their positions and now he'd be inside. He'd take his time. He'd make sure he held the high ground and wanted to take me by surprise. If he found the place empty, he'd have to revise his thinking. But first he'd make sure. He would have found the car in the back, so we weren't far off. He'd realize that I couldn't move fast with Velda and that I sure wouldn't leave her.

So he'd search. First the rooms, then for less obvious places.

I was running like hell, the .45 in my hand. I got to the house and stayed on the grass, edging to the back. The lock would have been easy enough for a pro to open. Or he could have knocked a pane out of the door window, reached in and turned the knob. That didn't matter. What mattered was that he was *in there*.

My feet felt the gravel and I stepped over it, got to the window and pushed it up. This was the one time I could die in a hurry, but the window went easily, he wasn't in the room and I slid in as silently as my shadow.

In the living room the firelight was dancing, throwing a dull orange glow over the place, the sound of the logs burning obscuring any small sounds I might have heard. I stepped out into the weird patterns the fire was making on the walls, listened again, then got down almost to my knees and started an animal crawl across the room.

The beam of a pencil flash made a quick splash of light around the corner. Then I heard it, the drag of chair legs across the floor. A hand suddenly slammed against the ceiling and he laughed. The bastard laughed!

I went in just as I heard a muffled scream from Velda and there in the dim, weaving light patterns were a pair of male legs sticking down from the attic opening, slowly going up as he raised himself with his arms.

For a second I was going to snatch him down. I changed my mind.

I cocked the .45, took real deliberate aim and touched the trigger. The gun blasted into a roaring yellowish light and for that one second I saw the leg jerk and twitch with a grotesque motion, and even before he could scream, I did it again to the other leg and the whole man came tumbling out of the ceiling opening, his hand still holding onto Velda, pulling her down with him.

My foot kicked him to one side, and I pulled Velda to her feet so we both could look down at Bradley. The impact of the slugs had shocked him almost breathless. Then the pain really hit him. His hands reached out, clawing wildly. He looked up at me with eyes so full of hate they seemed nearly black.

Quietly, I said, "He was your brother, wasn't he?"

He started to go wild then, thrashing his body in fury and pain, still trying to drag himself away. He was leaving a trail of blood behind and his face was tight with a screaming grimace. "My twin, you bastard! You killed my twin brother. You killed me, you rotten . . ."

I leaned down and put the muzzle of the .45 directly against Bradley's forehead. "If I do," I told him, "I'll cut off more than your fingers, Penta. I'll do it with your own knife."

Velda was standing there, not interfering, coldly observing.

I said, "There's a CB radio in the car, doll. The state troopers guard Channel Nine. Call them."

She nodded once and went to the door.

I was grinning down at Bradley. I wondered what the State Department was going to say. In a way it was too bad he was going back alive. The publicity was going to be terrible. It was going to louse up the big story that would put the NYPD on top and give Ray Wilson a glory sendoff and make Candace president some day.

The grin got to him. I was grinning at him the way I had at his brother back in the courtroom. Suddenly his body wrenched into spasms. He started ripping his clothes and screamed, "You killed me!" He glanced down and was ripping at his clothes again and screamed, "You killed me!"

"Not yet," I told him. He tried to twitch his head away from the gun, but I held it on him. He had thrashed around so he was pointing away from me, blood spatters streaking the wall. I felt some of it on my face and grinned again.

His hands were trying to reach his shattered legs, the agony foaming at his mouth. He saw my grin again and choked out another scream, making it into words. "You killed my brother and you killed me!"

Then he found the small-caliber pistol his hands had really been groping for and brought it up in a sweeping, deadly arc, one finger tightening around the trigger.

There was one smashing roar of the .45. His blood went all over the place. Fresh specks of crimson were on the back of my hand. I stood up slowly and gave him a hard grin he couldn't see any more.

I said, *"Now* I killed you, you shit."

For more than forty years Mickey Spillane's Mike Hammer novels have riveted people to their seats. Every one of his best-selling blockbusters is available in Signet paperback, including the special Fortieth Anniversary editions of these six classics:

I, The Jury

Vengeance Is Mine

My Gun Is Quick

One Lonely Night

The Big Kill

Kiss Me, Deadly

MY GUN IS QUICK

is Mike Hammer at his rugged best. He's out for blood when he sets off to nail the killer of a gorgeous redhead—a girl who played the wrong side of the street once too often. . . .

Here are a few pages of this sizzling best-seller with all the power of a knock-out punch!

I don't know how the place got by the health inspectors, because it stunk. There were two bums down at one end of the counter taking their time about finishing a ten-cent bowl of soup; making the most out of the free crackers and catsup in front of them. Halfway down a drunk concentrated between his plate of eggs and hanging on to the stool to keep from falling off the world. Evidently he was down to his last buck, for all his pockets had been turned inside out to locate the lone bill that was putting a roof on his load.

Until I sat down and looked in the mirror behind the shelves of pie segments, I didn't notice the fluff sitting off to one side at a table. She had red hair that didn't come out of a bottle, and looked pretty enough from where I was sitting.

The counterman came up just then and asked, "What'll it be?" He had a voice like a frog.

"Coffee. Black."

The fluff noticed me then. She looked up, smiled, tucked her nail tools in a peeling plastic handbag and hipped it in my direction. When she sat down on the stool next to me she nodded toward the counterman and said, "Shorty's got a heart of steel, mister. Won't even trust me for a cup of joe until I get a job. Care to finance me to a few vitamins?"

I was too tired to argue the point. "Make it two, feller." He grabbed another cup disgustedly and filled it, then set the two down on the counter, slopping half of it across the wash-worn linoleum top.

"Listen, Red," he croaked, "quit using this joint fer an office. First thing I got the cops on my tail. That's all I need."

"Be good and toddle off, Shorty. All I want from the gentleman is a cup of coffee. He looks much too tired to play any games tonight."

"Yeah, scram, Shorty," I put in. He gave me a nasty look, but since I was as ugly as he was and twice as big, he shuffled off to keep count over the cracker bowl in front of the bums. Then I looked at the redhead.

She wasn't very pretty after all. She had been once, but there are those things that happen under the skin and are reflected in the eyes and set of the mouth that take all the beauty out of a woman's face. Yeah, at one time she must have been almost beautiful. That wasn't too long ago, either. Her clothes were last year's old look and a little too tight. They showed a lot of leg and a lot of chest; nice white flesh still firm and young, but her face was old with knowledge that never came out of books. I watched her from the corner of my eye when she lifted her cup of coffee. She had delicate hands, long fingers tipped with deep-toned nails perfectly kept. It was the way she held the cup that annoyed me. Instead of being a thick, cracked mug, she gave it a touch of elegance as she balanced it in front of her lips. I thought she was wearing a wedding band until she put the cup down. Then I saw that it was just a ring with a fleur-de-lis design of blue enamel and diamond chips that had turned sideways slightly.

Red turned suddenly and said, "Like me?"

I grinned. "Uh-huh. But, like you said, much too tired to make it matter."

Her laugh was a tinkle of sound. "Rest easy, mister, I won't give you a sales talk. There are only certain types interested in what I have to sell."

"Amateur psychologist?"

"I have to be."

"And I don't look the type?"

Red's eyes danced. "Big mugs like you never have to pay, mister. With you it's the woman who pays."

I pulled out a deck of Luckies and offered her one. When we lit up I said, "I wish all the babes I met thought that way."

She blew a stream of smoke toward the ceiling and looked at me as if she were going back a long way. "They do, mister. Maybe you don't know it, but they do."

I don't know why I liked the kid. Maybe it was because she had eyes that were hard but could still cry a little. Maybe it was because she handed me some words that were nice to listen to. Maybe it was because I was tired and my cave was a cold, empty place, while here I had a redhead to talk to. Whatever it was, I liked her and she knew it and smiled at me in a way I knew she hadn't smiled in a long time. Like I was her friend.

"What's your name, mister?"

"Mike. Mike Hammer. Native-born son of ye old city presently at loose ends and dead tired. Free, white, and over twenty-one. That do it?"

"Well, what do you know! Here I've been thinking all males were named Smith or Jones. What happened?"

"No wife to report to, kid," I grinned. "That tag's my own. What do they call you besides Red?"

"They don't."

I saw her eyes crinkle a little as she sipped the last of her coffee. Shorty was casting nervous glances between us and the steamed-up window, probably hoping a cop wouldn't pass by and nail a hustler trying to make time. He gave me a pain.

"Want more coffee?"

She shook her head. "No, that did it fine. If Shorty wasn't so touchy about extending a little credit I wouldn't have to be smiling for my midnight snacks."

From the way I turned and looked at her, Red knew there was more than casual curiosity back of the remark when I asked, "I didn't think your line of business could ever be that slow."

For a brief second she glared into the mirror. "Is isn't." She was plenty mad about something.

I threw a buck on the counter and Shorty rang it up, then passed the change back. When I pocketed it I said to Red, "Did you ever stop to think that you're a pretty nice girl? I've met all kinds, but I think you could get along pretty well ... any way you tried."

Her smile even brought out a dimple that had been buried a long while ago. She kissed her finger, then touched the finger to my cheek. "I like that Mike. There are times when I think I've lost the power to like anyone, but I like you."

An el went by overhead just then and muffled the sound of the door opening. I felt the guy standing behind us before I saw him in the mirror. He was tall, dark and greasy-looking, with a built-in sneer that passed for knowhow, and he smelled of cheap hair oil. His suit would have been snappy in Harlem, edged with sharp pleats and creases.

He wasn't speaking to me when he said, "Hello, kid."

The redhead half turned and her lips went tight. "What do you want?" Her tone was dull, flat. The skin across her cheeks was drawn taut.

"Are you kidding?"

"I'm busy. Get lost."

The guy's hand shot out and grabbed her arm, swinging her around on the stool to face him. "I don't like them snotty remarks, Red."

As soon as I slid off the stool Shorty hustled down to our end, his hand reaching for something under the counter. When he saw my face he put it back and stopped short. The guy saw the same thing, but he was wise about it. His lip curled up and he snarled, "Get the hell out of here before I bust ya one."

He was going to make a pass at me, but I jammed four big, stiff fingers into his gut right above the navel and he snapped shut like a jack-knife. I opened him up again with an open-handed slap that left a blush across his mouth that was going to stay for a while.

Usually a guy will let it go right there. This one didn't. He could hardly breathe, but he was cursing me with his lips and his hand reached for his armpit in uncontrollable jerks. Red stood with her hand pressed against her mouth, while Shorty was croaking for us to cut it out, but too scared to move.

I let him almost reach it, then I slid my own .45 out where everybody could get a look at it. Just for effect I stuck it up against his forehead and thumbed back the hammer. It made a sharp click in the silence. "Just touch that rod you got and I'll blow your damned greasy head off. Go ahead, just make one lousy move toward it," I said.

He moved, all right. He fainted. Red was looking down at him, still too terrified to say anything. Shorty had a twitch in his shoulder. Finally she said, "You . . . didn't have to do that for me. Please, get out of here before he wakes up. He'll . . . kill you!"

I touched her arm, gently. "Tell me something, Red. Do you really think he could?"

Look for My Gun Is Quick *in its special Fortieth Anniversary edition, along with five other classic Mike Hammer novels by Mickey Spillane.*

THE BIG KILL

*is blockbusting Spillane in which Mike Hammer
slugs it out with a vicious killer. The victim—a re-
formed ex-con who lost his chance to go straight
once and for all. . . .*

*Here are a few pages from the brawl-packed, bullet-
paced thriller, as only Mickey Spillane can deliver.*

It was one of those nights when the sky came
down and wrapped itself around the world. The
rain clawed at the windows of the bar like an
angry cat and tried to sneak in every time some
drunk lurched in the door. The place reeked of
stale beer and soggy men with enough cheap
perfume thrown in to make you sick.

Two drunks with a nickel between them were
arguing over what to play on the jukebox until a
tomato in a dress that was too tight a year ago
pushed the key that started off something noisy
and hot. One of the drunks wanted to dance and
she gave him a shove. So he danced with the
other drunk.

She saw me sitting there with my stool tipped
back against the cigarette machine and change of
a fin on the bar, decided I could afford a wet

evening for two, and walked over with her hips waving hello.

"You're new around here, ain't ya?"

"Nah. I've been here since six o'clock."

"Buy me a drink?" She crowded in next to me, seeing how much of herself she could plaster against my legs.

"No." It caught her by surprise and she quit rubbing.

"Don't gentlemen usually buy ladies a drink?" she said. She tried to lower her eyelids seductively, but one came down farther than the other and made her look stupid.

"I'm not a gentleman, kid."

"I ain't a lady either so buy me a drink."

So I bought her a drink. A jerk in a discarded army overcoat down at the end of the bar was getting the eye from the bartender because he was nursing the last drop in his glass, hating to go outside in the rain, so I bought him a drink too.

The bartender took my change with a frown. "Them bums'll bleed you to death, feller."

"I don't have any blood left," I told him. The dame grinned and rubbed herself against my knees some more.

"I bet you got plenty of everything for me."

"Yeah, but what I got you ain't getting because you probably got more than me."

"What?"

"Forget it."

She looked at my face a second, then edged away. "You ain't very sociable, mister."

"I know it. I don't want to be sociable. I haven't been sociable the last six months and I won't be for the next six if I can help it."

"Say, what's eatin' you? You having dame trouble?"

"I never have dame trouble. I'm a misanthropist."

"You *are?*" Her eyes widened as if I had something contagious. She finished her drink and was going to stick it out anyway, no matter what I said.

I said, "Scram."

This time she scowled a little bit. "Say, what the hell's eatin' you? I never—"

"I don't like people. I don't like any kind of people. When you get them together in a big lump they all get nasty and dirty and full of trouble. So I don't like people, including you. That's what a misanthropist is."

"I coulda sworn you was a nice feller," she said.

"So could a lot of people. I'm not. Blow, sister."

She gave me a look she kept in reserve for special occasions and got the hell out of there so I could drink by myself. It was a stinking place to have to spend the night, but that's all there was on the block. The East Side doesn't cater to the uptown trade. I sat there and watched the clock go around, waiting for the rain to stop, but it was as patient as I was. It was almost malicious the way it came down, a million fingers that drummed a constant, maddening tattoo on the windows until its steady insistence rose above the bawdy talk and raucous screams of the jukebox.

It got to everybody after a while, that and the smell of the damp. A fight started down at the other end and spread along the bar. It quit when the bartender rapped one guy over the head with an ice stick. One bum dropped his glass and got tossed out. The tomato who liked to rub herself had enough of it and picked up a guy who had enough left of his change to make the evening profitable and took him home in the rain. The guy didn't like it, but biology got the better of common sense again.

And I got a little bit drunk. Not much, just a little bit.

But enough so that in about five minutes I knew damn well I was going to get sick of the whole mess and start tossing them the hell out the door. Maybe the bartender too if he tried to use the stick on me. Then I could drink in peace and the hell with the rain.

Oh, I felt swell, just great.

I kept looking around to see where I'd start first, then the door opened and shut behind a guy who stood there in his shirtsleeves, wet and shivering. He had a bundle in his arms with his coat over it, and when he quit looking around the place like a scared rabbit he shuffled over to one of the booths and dropped the bundle on the seat.